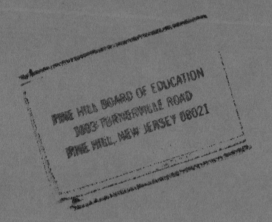

The Century Kids

THE 1930s

Directions

BEVERLY HILLS LOS ANGELES
HOLLYWOOD

TRIPS TO THE
HOMES OF
MOVIE
STARS

Lets Go Places
with RICHFIELD

by Dorothy and Tom Hoobler

The Millbrook Press • Brookfield, Connecticut

Photographs courtesy of Bison Archives: pp. 3, 141, 142;
Private collections: pp. 8 (Leo), 9 (Tony), 12 (Gabriella);
Library of Congress: p. 22; UPI/Corbis-Bettmann: pp. 28, 56,
74, 75, 91, 98, 99, 149; Underwood Photo Archives: pp. 6, 7,
14, 18, 30, 47, 70, 154 (William, Anna, Harry, Jack, Sara, Peggy,
Charles, Nell, Esther), 155 (Maud, Nick, Polly); Chicago
Historical Society (ICHi-26098): p. 38; Bettmann/Corbis: pp. 42,
116; Culver Pictures, Inc.: pp. 50, 96; © Nabisco: p. 67;
Corbis/Underwood & Underwood: p. 85; FDR Library:
p. 126; Hulton Getty/Liaison Agency: p. 129;
© Milton Bradley: p. 146

In Memory of Elaine Law Long

Library of Congress Cataloging-in-Publication Data
Hoobler, Dorothy.
The 1930s: directions/by Dorothy and Tom Hoobler.
p. cm.–(The century kids)
Summary: In the summer of 1936, Tony runs away from his home
above his family's Italian restaurant in Chicago, while in Berlin David
is present at the Olympics and prepares to move to America.
ISBN 0-7613-1603-5 (lib. bdg.)
1. Depressions–1929–Juvenile fiction. 2. Olympic Games (11th: 1936:
Berlin, Germany)–Juvenile fiction. [1. Depressions–1929–Fiction.
2. Olympic Games (11th: 1936: Berlin, Germany)–Fiction. 3. Berlin
(Germany)–Fiction. 4. Germany–Fiction. 5. Runaways–Fiction.]
I. Hoobler, Thomas. II. Title.
Pz7.H76227 Fo 2000
[Fic]–dc21   00-026513

Published by The Millbrook Press, Inc.
2 Old New Milford Road
Brookfield, Connecticut 06804
www.millbrookpress.com

A Radio Show

JULY 25, 1936

"COME OVER HERE, TONY," SAID POP. "YOU TOO, Leo. I want you to meet an old friend of mine."

Leo peered out from behind the stack of freshly washed tablecloths he was carrying. The truck driver from the laundry had wanted somebody to pay the bill, but he and Tony had talked him into waiting another day or two.

"Maybe this is somebody who could float Pop a loan," Leo said in a low voice.

Tony shook his head. Nobody would be that dumb. The restaurant business wasn't worth a plugged nickel. People just weren't going out to eat any more. They couldn't afford it. Lots of families didn't even have anything to eat at home.

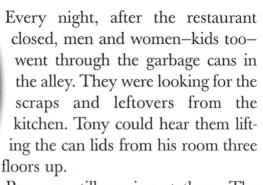

Rocco

Every night, after the restaurant closed, men and women—kids too—went through the garbage cans in the alley. They were looking for the scraps and leftovers from the kitchen. Tony could hear them lifting the can lids from his room three floors up.

Pop was still waving at them. The man with him had light brown hair that was getting thin in places.

"Freddy," Pop said, "these are my two no-good sons." He smiled. "Boys, Freddy and I listened to the last messages from the *Titanic* back in 1912."

"That was my first wireless set," said Freddy. "We sat up for two or three days straight, didn't we, Rocco?"

Tony and Leo looked at each other. They had not heard this story before. "Was this when you lived with the old movie star?" Leo asked.

"Freddy is Nell's cousin," said Pop. "And she isn't old. She's just as beautiful as ever. Isn't she, Freddy?"

Freddy nodded. "I saw her last summer," he said. "I wanted her to come on the radio, but nothing doing."

"Freddy is the head of programming for CBN—the Central Broadcasting Network," Pop told the boys. "And what do you think?"

The boys waited. Pop was always asking them what they thought, but he didn't really want to know. He'd tell them soon enough.

"He's going to broadcast a program from right here in the restaurant."

They were surprised. "You mean like the shows they do in New York?" Tony asked. "With an orchestra and music?"

Freddy

Pop smiled. "Sure, it will be just like before the Depression."

"Who's gonna pay for that, Pop?" Tony asked.

A year ago, the restaurant had to let go the musicians that played every night at dinner. Mom had finally told Pop they just couldn't afford them anymore.

Pop ignored Tony's question. "We can get most of the old orchestra back," Pop said. "They haven't found new jobs yet."

"Does Mom know about this?" Tony asked.

"Don't you worry about that," Pop replied. His face turned angry then, the way it did so often these past few years. "Just don't say anything about this for now. I shouldn't have told you, but I thought you'd be excited."

Pop looked around the empty dining room. "I thought you two were supposed to put the

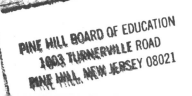

7

clean tablecloths on the tables," he said. "Go on, get to it."

The boys went back to work. When they were far enough away so Pop couldn't hear them, Tony said, "I'm sick of all this."

"Aw, don't worry," Leo told his older brother. Even though Tony was 13, and one year older, he was a hothead and Leo often had to calm him down. "Pop's just trying to make things the way they used to be."

"That's just it," Tony replied. "He acts like nothing's changed. The whole country's gone broke, and he wants to have dancing and music in here. We haven't even got any customers."

"It isn't as bad as that," Leo said. "Some people still come by, you know that. Maybe having a radio program here would be a good idea. It could attract more customers."

Leo

"Why?" asked Tony. "They can listen at home for free."

Leo nodded. Tony was as hard to argue with as Pop. But Leo felt Pop was right to be trying something.

Tony snapped open a folded tablecloth, and Leo caught the other end as they laid it over a table. Smoothing down the wrinkles, Tony added,

"Instead of hiring back the musicians, Pop ought to be letting go some more waiters. We don't need half the people working here."

"He can't do that," Leo said quietly. "Some of them have been with him for years. They couldn't find other jobs. Pop thinks of them as part of our family."

"What about Lorraine?" Tony said.

Tony

Leo was shocked. "Tony, Lorraine's like our older sister. Her mother took care of us all the time we were growing up. Mom showed Lorraine how to cook so she could take a little time off. Even Pop says Lorraine cooks well enough to be Italian. And she needs her job as bad as anybody. She has to pay tuition at the University of Chicago."

"Why does she need to go to college?" asked Tony. "I'm never going to go there, I know that."

Leo bit his lip to keep himself from saying anything more. Tony had a lot of trouble at school. Not because he wasn't smart. He was restless and had a hard time paying attention. Somehow, what the teachers said didn't have much effect on him. His mind was always somewhere else.

Tony's poor grades made Pop upset. He always reminded his sons that they had an advantage he didn't. They could go to school. "The only real education I got," said Pop, "was the summer I spent with Nell Aldrich's family. Her great-aunt taught me everything."

Of course, Tony's response was, "If that was good enough for you, why do we need any more education than that?" Pop had no answer, but he had his heart set on Leo and Tony going to college.

Leo didn't mind for himself, although he noticed that going to college hadn't helped a lot of people who were hurt by the Depression. There was a man selling apples on the corner near the restaurant. He once told Leo he had graduated from Harvard with three degrees in economics. "I used to work as a stock analyst," the man said. "Until the stock market crashed."

"What went wrong?" Leo asked him.

"It was really very simple," the man said. "It was fear, just like President Roosevelt said. When the price of stocks started to go down, everybody sold, and prices went down further. Even people who didn't own stocks got worried and stopped spending money. So that threw others out of work, and they couldn't earn money. After that, things just got worse."

Leo didn't understand that, but it sounded interesting. He felt if he went to college he might be able to figure it out.

Tony said something that made Leo stop day-dreaming. "That silent movie star Nell Aldrich that Pop says he used to know . . . do you remember her?"

"Oh, sure," Leo said. "She used to come in once in a while when we were little. She hasn't been here for a long time, though."

"Where does she live now, anyway?"

"I don't know . . . why? California, I guess. Hollywood. Ask Pop."

"I don't want to ask him," Tony replied.

"What do you want to know for?"

"No reason. Just forget I asked. Don't mention it to anybody."

"This guy who's putting on the radio show—he would know," Leo said. "He's related to her."

Tony shook his head and plopped down the last of the tablecloths. "I'll finish up here," he said. "Why don't you see if Mom needs somebody to watch Gabriella? Mom ought to be getting things started in the kitchen."

"Lorraine will do it."

"This is Wednesday," said Tony. "Lorraine's not coming in till late. She's got a night class. Or at least she says."

Leo nodded. As he left the main dining room, he saw workers bringing in long rolls of rubber cable. It made him a little worried. I hope having a radio show here isn't going to mess up the restaurant, he thought.

Upstairs, he found Mom asleep in a chair and Gabriella on the floor playing with her two Shirley Temple dolls. Gabriella looked up when he came in and put a finger to her lips. She made a loud shushing sound with her eyes wide. "Babies are asleep," she whispered.

Leo laughed and picked her up. "You take good care of the babies, don't you?" he asked.

She nodded, shaking her dark brown curls that Mom had made to look just like Shirley Temple's.

"Shall we wake up Mom?" he asked.

A firm shake no.

"Then who's going to cook?"

Gabriella

"I'll cook," Gabriella piped up. She pointed to her tiny set of china cups and dishes. "I cook good."

"I'll bet you do," Leo said. "But you're only three, so you'd need a lot of help."

"You help me," she suggested.

"No, Mom will show you someday," he told her.

Gabriella shook her head again. "She does it too hard," she said.

"What? Mom cooks hard?"

Gabriella patiently tried to explain it.

"When she cooks, it's too hard." She pointed to Mom asleep. "That's why she's tired."

Leo nodded. Even Gabriella could see that Mom worked too hard. Back when Leo and Tony were Gabriella's age, Mom had hired Mrs. Dixon to help take care of them. But Mrs. Dixon and her husband had moved to Detroit by the time Gabriella was born. So Mom said she had "decided to have the fun of raising my own daughter by myself."

Only it was too much work for her, even with Mrs. Dixon's daughter Lorraine helping in the kitchen. Mom still got up early to go to the food markets. She wouldn't trust anybody else to pick out the vegetables, fruit, and meat—even the eggs, cream, and cheese. Leo once asked Mom what made one egg better than another. She said it was the way the shell felt to her. She couldn't teach it to anybody.

Anyway, since Lorraine would be late tonight somebody had to start cooking. Leo touched Mom on the arm, and she opened her eyes at once. "Check the pasta," she said. "Don't let it get overdone."

"It's OK, Mom," Leo said. "Dinner hasn't started yet."

"What time is it?" she asked.

"It's only four-thirty," he told her.

She relaxed and closed her eyes.

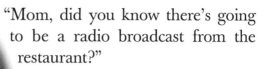

Mom

"Mom, did you know there's going to be a radio broadcast from the restaurant?"

She opened one eye and peered at him suspiciously. "We've had a radio in the kitchen for years," she said. "But I would not like to have one in the dining rooms. Restaurants that play radios seem cheap to me. Live music is classy, but the radio . . ."

"No, Mom," said Leo. "I mean a program. CBN is going to have somebody broadcast a program right from our restaurant."

She closed her eye and sighed. "That was Freddy's idea, wasn't it? When he called your father, I knew it was trouble."

"Yes, he was here. He said it would bring people into the restaurant. Don't you think it will?"

"We'll see," she said. "Things couldn't get much worse, that's for sure."

Leo wasn't so certain of that.

The Host of the Show

JULY 28, 1936

THE WAITERS KEPT COMPLAINING ABOUT THE cables. Even though they were taped to the floor, they were easy to trip over—particularly if you were carrying a tray with half a dozen dishes of hot food on it.

Pop had to admit it was a problem. Especially after he had to apologize to three customers and pay to have their suits cleaned when plates of linguine with white clam sauce came crashing down on them.

"At this rate," Tony said to Leo, "by the time the radio show starts, we'll have killed the last of the customers we have."

Unfortunately, Pop heard him and that set off another fight. Pop must really have been angry, because he started shouting in Italian. What he said, Leo couldn't understand, but even the waiters looked shocked.

Finally, Tony threw up his hands and stormed off. Leo started to go after him, but Mom caught his arm. "Let him cool off," she said. "It's better if he and your pop aren't in the same room for a while."

"I don't like to see them fight," Leo told her. "I've tried to get Tony to just go along with Pop's ideas, but he has to argue."

"They're too much alike," Mom told him.

"They don't seem alike to me," said Leo.

"You didn't know your pop when he was Tony's age," Mom replied. "He was eager. He had to grow up fast."

"Tony's ready to quit school and start working full time," said Leo. "He could help the restaurant a lot."

"I know," said Mom. "But Rocco has other dreams for Tony. He thinks . . . well, never mind what he thinks."

Mom's face got a look that Leo recognized. It appeared whenever she was thinking about the Aldrich family. Long ago, when Pop first came to the United States, he lived with the Aldriches for a few months. He was friends with Nell Aldrich, who was the same age as Pop. Later, she became a big movie star, although she hadn't made any movies in a long time. Right now her cousin Harry was a lot more famous. He had been an automobile race driver back in the 1920s, and then went into the movies. People said he did his own stunts.

Pop was proud of knowing the Aldriches. But whenever one of them dropped by the restaurant on a visit to Chicago, Mom seemed a little upset. Not angry exactly. Just not the same warm person she was around everybody else. Leo wondered if the reason had to do with Nell Aldrich. He shrugged off the thought. He had to get his math homework done so he could be downstairs in the restaurant tonight. The first radio broadcast would start at eight o'clock, and he wasn't going to miss it.

Leo was a little surprised when he saw the host of the program. At first he thought it must be a messenger boy. But of course no messenger would be dressed in a double-breasted brown suit with a white carnation in the lapel. And a green tie with a pink shirt. The thing was, he looked very young—much too young to have a radio show.

He was fat too, although of course that didn't matter much on the radio. It all depended on what you sounded like. Leo's favorite radio show was *The Shadow*. The Shadow was a crime fighter who could make himself invisible. In real life, he was Lamont Cranston, a wealthy young man-about-town. He could make himself invisible by clouding men's minds—a secret he had learned in the Orient. But Leo didn't have to see the Shadow to know what he looked like. He had a picture of him in his mind from the way he sounded on the radio.

"Is that Charley?" This voice was Pop's. He came up to the chubby young man in the double-breasted suit and shook his hand. "Hello, Rocco," the man replied.

"I thought you were in college," Pop said. "Harvard or someplace like that?"

"I started," Charley said. "I didn't mind going to the classes, but it was too distracting to have to study for tests. So when Uncle Freddy offered me a chance to do a radio show, I couldn't refuse."

Leo smiled to himself as he heard this. He'd have to tell Tony to try using that excuse.

Charley

"What kind of show is this going to be?" Pop asked.

"I thought I'd interview people," Charley replied.

"Interview?" Pop sounded puzzled.

"You know, talk to them about what they do. I figure I have enough interesting relatives to get started. After that, I'll invite other people of talent or accomplishment."

"You going to have Nell on the show?" Pop looked toward the doorway as if he hoped to see her come through.

"No . . . she's sort of fallen out of the public eye," Charley told him. "My cousin Molly said she would drop in and bring a friend of hers. Molly's going to coach the American women's track team at the Olympics."

Pop looked uneasy. "And you're just going to . . . talk?"

Charley nodded.

"I don't know if that will be enough."

"Oh, we can easily fill an hour just chatting," Charley said. "There are commercials too, so we really have only about forty-five minutes."

"But I mean, shouldn't you tell jokes? Have people sing? We hired an orchestra. Freddy was sure you'd have some musical numbers."

Charley thought about it. "No . . ." he said slowly, ". . . music might be too distracting."

"What am I going to do with the musicians?" Pop asked. "At least you'll need music to begin and end the show, won't you?" He looked desperate. "A theme song?"

Charley shook his head. "I've already thought of that," he said. "I have something novel and amusing planned."

Pop made a noise that sounded like the machine in the kitchen that crushed ice. He turned and walked away in a hurry. As he passed Leo, he said, "Have you seen Freddy?" but went on before Leo could answer.

Charley gave no sign that he thought anything was wrong. He caught Leo's eye. "Could you show me where the microphone has been set up?" he asked.

Leo led him to the table near what was to be the orchestra stand. Charley stumbled on one of the cables and said indignantly, "That's a foolish thing to have where people are walking."

Even though it was the height of the early dinner hour, most of the tables in the dining room were empty. A couple of people looked up curiously at Charley, and then went back to their dinners.

"Can I bring you something to eat?" Leo asked.

"For now, I'd like a pitcher of water and a glass. No ice, please."

As Leo returned with the water, he saw that Charley had opened a book. Pop wouldn't like that either. Nobody even read a newspaper while they were eating at Rocco's. If somebody came in alone, Pop would come over and make conversation at their table. "Talking at meals helps digestion," he said. "Otherwise, you eat too fast."

So after Leo put down the glass and poured water into it, he waited. Charley looked up from his book and said, "Does Lorraine Dixon still work here?"

"Yes," Leo replied. "But she's not in right now. She has a class."

"A class? In what? Typing? Shorthand?"

"I don't think so," Leo replied. "She's at the University of Chicago. She wants to go to law school."

Charley's eyebrows rose. "Is that so? Hm. Did she ever tell you about the time she helped me apprehend a jewel thief?"

Leo stared at him. The way Leo had heard it, Lorraine had practically caught the thief all by herself.

Just then Pop came back. He still looked angry. "I can't find Freddy," he said. "The musicians have arrived. I have to pay them, so you must find something for them to do."

Charley motioned to the bandstand behind him. "Let them come in, if you insist," he said. "We may have a musical interlude."

Pop caught sight of Leo. "Where's your brother?" he asked sharply.

"I guess he's upstairs."

"Customers are here," Pop said, gesturing around the nearly empty room. "Why isn't he helping? Go find him."

Leo wanted to stay and see how the show got on the air. But he could tell Pop was upset, so off he went.

He found Tony up in their room. He was lying on his bed reading *Black Mask*, a magazine that

printed detective and adventure stories. Tony's schoolbooks sat unopened on the floor.

"Pop's looking for you," said Leo. "The radio show's about to start."

Tony didn't look up. "Turn on our radio," he said. "Let's see how it sounds."

Squeals and hisses came out of the second-hand Crosley table radio the boys had bought from a junk shop. Leo fiddled with the tuning knob. At last they heard the somewhat scratchy voice of a studio announcer: "And now, direct to you from the world-famous Rocco's Restaurant on Chicago's North Side . . . "

"World-famous!" Tony said with a snicker. Leo shushed him.

". . . It's the Charley Norman Show!"

Silence followed, and then a faint tinkly noise. "What's that?" asked Tony. "Where's the orchestra?"

Leo raised his hand, trying to shush Tony so he could hear.

Then came Charley's voice. "That," he said, "was the sound of an heirloom musical watch originally owned by my great-grandfather Lionel Aldrich."

"What happened to the *orchestra*?" Tony asked again.

"He didn't want one," Leo said. Tony stared at him.

"I wanted you to hear it," Charley's voice went on, "because it reminds me of something we all ought to remember in the tough times we're facing now."

Tony shot a quizzical look at Leo. Leo spread his hands and shrugged.

Suddenly Leo realized something. Over the radio, Charley sounded good. You didn't think of a chubby kid when you heard him. Instead, you thought you were listening to a man-about-town, like Lamont Cranston, the Shadow. Leo was so surprised, he let out a laugh.

"What's funny?" Tony said.

Charley's voice went on describing what the watch made him think of: " . . . old-fashioned values, courage in the face of adversity, belief in the future . . ."

"What kind of program *is* this?" asked Tony.

"And tonight," said Charley, "we're going to be talking with a couple of people about those values. My cousin Molly Aldrich Woods and a friend she's brought with her. The famous aviatrix Amelia Earhart."

"Wow, Amelia Earhart!" said Leo. "The first woman to fly across the Atlantic Ocean. Let's go downstairs and see her, Tony."

"You go," said Tony. "I don't feel like it."

Leo hesitated. "Tony, Pop sent me up here to bring you downstairs."

"What for? Is the place full of people?"

Leo shook his head. "Same as always," he admitted. "But maybe if people hear the program, it could help. People might want to come in and see what's going on."

"In a pig's eye," replied Tony.

Leo shrugged. There wasn't anything else he could do. He went back downstairs wondering what he should tell Pop.

THREE

Why Not Now?

JULY 28, 1936

AFTER LEO HAD LEFT, TONY TOSSED ASIDE THE *Black Mask* magazine. His head was full of dreams. He was tired of doing nothing all day in school and then coming home to pretend that the restaurant would be full of people that night.

He wanted to get out of here. A few months ago, a customer had left a book in the cloakoom. He never came back for it, and out of curiosity Tony started to read it. It was called *New Worlds to Conquer*, written by a man named Richard Halliburton.

Halliburton traveled to new places all over the world. He went wherever he liked, stopping as long as he wanted. Something interesting and

NEW WORLDS TO CONQUER

Richard Halliburton

Author of THE ROYAL ROAD TO ROMANCE *and* THE GLORIOUS ADVENTURE

exciting always seemed to happen to him. The people he met were more fascinating than anybody Tony knew.

Tony found out that Halliburton had written other books. He went to the library and read them too. It seemed to him that living like Halliburton was about the best life anybody could have.

Why not get started now? The thought ran through Tony's head more and more often. He'd saved over fifteen dollars from tips, without telling anybody.

Really, he was just taking up space here. If he stayed, he would be nothing but a waiter all his life. Taking orders from fat people who complained a lot and acted like it was a big deal if they gave you a quarter for a tip.

Why not get started now? Whenever he thought about it, he could think of reasons why not. For one thing, he needed to have a destination in mind. That was the way Halliburton did it. He set out heading for some exotic place, but it was the journey–getting there–that was the real fun.

Now, Tony had a destination. Tony and Leo had always heard about Nell Aldrich. Pop liked to talk about her, but Tony wondered if they were really such good friends. There was one way to find out. He'd go out to Hollywood, find out where she lived, knock on the door, and say, "I'm Rocco Vivanti's son." If she let him in and invited him to stay for dinner, that would prove they really had been friends. If not . . . Tony would have the laugh on Pop.

Why not get started right now? Tony got up and opened a dresser drawer. Halliburton always said to travel light. Wherever you went, you could find what you needed. He picked out an extra pair of pants, a couple of shirts, underwear, socks . . . He stuffed everything into a duffel bag and lifted it. It wasn't too heavy.

Mom would be upset.

Tony knew that. It was another of the things that stopped him before now. Pop would probably pretend to be upset, but after a day or two he'd say something in Italian that meant, "Forget about him if he wants to play cards with the devil." Pop had a lot of old Italian sayings to use whenever something went wrong. Which was pretty often. But Mom would be upset. Tony knew that. He sighed and put the copy of *Black Mask* into the duffel bag. Maybe he'd write her a letter.

Downstairs, Leo stood against the wall of the dining room watching. Pop was sitting at a table next to the one where Charley and his guests were. He looked like he had forgotten about being angry. In fact, he was listening intently to the program.

Amelia Earhart was talking about flying, "It's a feeling like no other," she said. "You've escaped the earth, and it seems like you've left all your cares and troubles behind you. Have you ever flown?"

"No," said Charley. "I must admit that I feel more secure in a train or automobile, knowing the wheels are planted firmly on the ground. I think I would attempt flying if the plane were very close to the ground—four to six feet, for instance."

Amelia Earhart laughed. Leo was struck by the way she looked, with a friendly, open face and her hair cut almost as short as a boy's. He thought she was beautiful. "Actually," she said, "you're much safer if the plane is high up. If the engine fails, you don't fall like a stone. You begin to glide, and you can search for a safe place to land."

"Unless you're over the ocean," Charley said.

She smiled. "True, but then it wouldn't help you if you were only four feet above the water."

"Well," he said, "I understand you're planning an even more spectacular flight than crossing the Atlantic."

"Next year, if everything goes well," she said. "I want to fly completely around the world."

Some of the people in the restaurant gasped, and others applauded.

"Not all at once, surely," Charley said.

"No, we'll be stopping at places along the way to refuel and take on supplies. But I think it can be accomplished in less than a week, which would be faster than anyone else has ever done it."

"You said we, so you're not going alone."

She nodded. "I'll need a navigator and someone to fly while I sleep. I wanted Molly here to go along, but she's too busy."

Charley turned to the other woman at the table. "Molly, what is it that's keeping you from flying around the world? I would think you'd jump at the chance."

"I would, Charley," she told him, "but coaching the women's Olympic track team is lots of work."

"The Olympics are starting soon, aren't they?"

Molly

"The opening ceremonies will be August 1, this Saturday. I'm taking a plane to Berlin tomorrow. As a matter of fact, Charley, I'll be visiting some of our relatives while I'm there, and maybe I'll even enter a golf tournament or two in Europe."

"Do you still play golf?" he asked. "And tennis?"

"Of course," she said, sounding surprised that he'd asked.

He pressed on. "No plans to retire?"

Molly turned to Amelia Earhart and said, "Say, will you listen to this guy?" They laughed.

Molly turned back and said, "If you're doing something you enjoy, what's the point of retiring? Oh, I can't hit a tennis ball as hard as I used to, but physical exercise and sports are something that people should pursue all their lives."

A ripple of applause came from the tables around the room. Leo noticed that people were enjoying the show.

"Tell us about your twin sister Polly," Charley said. Leo thought he looked eager to change the subject. "How long has it been since anyone has seen her?"

"A couple of years," Molly replied. "She and her husband went up the Amazon River in April or May of 1934."

"Have you thought of searching for her? Perhaps in an airplane?"

"Why?" asked Molly. "She knows the way back."

"Two years seems like an awfully long time to be in the jungle."

"It's a rain forest, as I'm sure she'd tell you. And really, she feels more at home there than she would here in Chicago."

"Why is that?"

"Because there are more insects there than any other place in the world."

A man in shirtsleeves and suspenders knelt in front of Charley's table and waved to him. "I see that it's time for a message from our sponsor," said Charley. "We'll be back for more chat in a little while. Stay tuned."

When the microphone had been turned off, Pop walked over to Charley's table. Leo came closer so he could hear.

"This show . . ." Pop said, gesturing with his hands, ". . . people enjoy it."

"Do you really think so?" said Charley, looking pleased.

"It could still use a little music," Pop suggested.

"I forgot," said Charley. He turned to look at the orchestra behind him. The musicians looked bored. Several had put down their instruments and were eating. "They can play something when we go back on the air," Charley said.

"And if you could . . ." Pop began.

"Yes?"

Pop leaned over and rubbed the fingers of his right hand together. He did that whenever he was thinking of money. "Mention the address of the restaurant in case people get lost."

Upstairs, Tony was working on a letter to his mother. So far, all he had written was

"DEAR MOM."

He was trying to decide if he should add, "AND POP." The radio was still on, and Tony suddenly noticed that music was coming from it. It worried him. Did that mean the program downstairs was over? If so, Leo would be back up here in a minute. If he found out what Tony intended to do, he'd try to talk him out of it.

Tony scrawled "AND POP" on the paper after all, and then added, "I'M GOING AWAY. DON'T WORRY."

He thought about adding, "I'LL BE BACK," but decided that showed what Richard Halliburton would have called "a want of determination." Instead he just finished with, "YOUR SON, TONY" at the bottom. Folding the paper, he slipped it under the door to his parents' room.

He stood in the hallway and looked around. The duffel bag suddenly felt heavier. His legs were shaky. Memories of good times he'd had in these rooms floated through his mind.

He shook his head to get rid of them.

Why not get started *right now?*

He closed the door quietly and went down the back stairs to the alley behind the restaurant. Somebody was there, and Tony shrank back for a second. But then he saw it wasn't anybody who worked for Pop. Just a bum searching the garbage cans for something to eat.

As Tony brushed by, he didn't notice that the bum was no older than he was. And even if he had noticed, he wouldn't have thought there was any chance that he'd be doing the same thing not very many weeks later.

FOUR

A Trick on Tony

SOMETHING WAS WRONG. LEO SENSED IT WHEN HE went back upstairs and didn't find Tony. He looked into Gabriella's room. Sometimes she woke up and wanted somebody to read a story to her. Usually Leo did that, but Tony might have.

Tony wasn't there, however, and Gabriella was fast asleep.

There was no reason for Tony to be out this late at night. Leo tried to remember what Tony was doing earlier. He remembered him reading *Black Mask*. He looked around for the magazine, even under the bed. It was gone. That was when Leo opened the bureau drawers. When he saw Tony's clothes missing, he knew.

35

He felt a sinking feeling in his stomach. Leo couldn't imagine what it would be like with Tony gone. It would be like losing an arm or a leg. Leo knew that maybe he was smarter than Tony, but Tony was always the leader of the two. Why would he do something like this? Leo thought of what Pop would say: *pazza*, crazy.

There wasn't anything to do. Leo crawled into bed and pulled the covers up. Maybe tomorrow morning Tony would be back.

Mom woke Leo around one o'clock in the morning. She didn't seem as upset as Leo thought she'd be, but that made her even scarier. She turned on the lamp and showed him Tony's note. "Did you know about this?" she asked.

"No, Mom, really," he said.

"He didn't tell you even where he was going?"

"No, he didn't say anything. We listened to the radio program up here for a while. Then I went downstairs. I didn't see him after that."

Mom nodded. Then she put her arms around Leo, surprising him. "Promise me you'll never do anything like this," she said.

"I promise, Mom," he told her.

"You're a good boy," she said. Letting him go, she sat thinking. "I don't know how I'm going to tell your pop."

"Pop?" Leo thought he must know already.

So when Pop finally locked up the restaurant and came upstairs, Leo watched closely. Pop's hands shook a little when he read the note, and then he crumpled it up and threw it on the floor. He said something to himself in Italian, and then shrugged.

"He'll be back," he said loudly. Looking at Leo, he said, "You know it's hard for people to earn enough money today, don't you?"

Leo nodded.

"You ever go hungry here? Ever have to wear torn clothes to school? Or shoes with cardboard stuffed into the bottom?"

"No, Pop."

"But you've seen people like that, yes?"

"Yes, Pop."

"So your brother wants to live with those kinds of people, let him. He finds out what that's like, he'll come crawling back." Leo said nothing. But he knew Pop didn't understand Tony at all.

Even Leo would have been surprised, however, to learn where Tony was at that very minute. After leaving the restaurant, Tony had taken the El to the Dearborn Avenue Railroad Station. He went inside and tried to find out when the next train left for Hollywood, California. Up on the wall were a couple of big boards with names of cities, but he did not see any that read "Hollywood."

Dearborn Avenue Railroad Station, Chicago

It was pretty empty in the station at this time of night. Tony felt self-conscious, as if everybody who went by was staring at him. So he was relieved when a tall, well-dressed man stopped and spoke kindly. The man had gray hair and was wearing a dark blue suit with a striped gray-and-yellow tie. "Young man," he said, "are you waiting to meet someone?"

"No, sir," Tony replied.

"Traveling by yourself, then? Where are you headed?"

"Well, I wanted to go to Hollywood, but I can't figure out what train to take."

"Hollywood," the man said with a grin, "You're planning to enter the movie business?"

"No," said Tony. "I'm just going out there to see if I can find someone."

"Well, the train you want is the one to Los Angeles," the man told him. "It's a long trip. Have you enough money for your ticket?"

"Yes, sir," Tony told him. "Fifteen dollars."

"I see. But you want to save as much of that as you can. The fare to Los Angeles is eleven dollars. If you're traveling alone, they'll charge you full fare, even if you're underage. That will leave you only four dollars for food and whatever expenses you might have after you arrive."

Tony swallowed hard. Maybe he should have saved up some more money. "I think I can make it on that," he said.

"I tell you what," the man said. "If I buy the ticket for you, I can say you're my son and get a half-price ticket. That will save you five fifty."

Tony nodded. That seemed like a good idea. He was lucky to have run into this man.

"Why don't you sit down here," the man said, "and watch my briefcase while I get the tickets?" He pointed to a brown case resting on the end of a bench nearby. "If the cashier sees how big you are, he might still charge full fare."

"Sure thing," Tony said. "I really appreciate this."

"Let me have your money," the man said. Tony pulled from his pocket a roll of one-dollar bills, held together by a rubber band. He started to slip off the band to count off six singles, but the man said, "Why don't you give me all of it for safe-keeping? The train station is full of pickpockets."

Tony hesitated for only a second before reminding himself that the man was doing him a big favor. He was grateful to have found someone who was so experienced at traveling. He handed over the money.

The man walked off toward the ticket counter. Tony decided to move a bit closer to his briefcase, so he could keep an eye on it. Dragging his duffel bag along he slid down the smooth wooden bench.

Not a moment too soon, either. For at the same time a stranger walked over and picked up the briefcase.

"Ah, excuse me," Tony said. "I'm watching that briefcase."

The stranger looked sharply at him. "Oh, you are? I guess you want a nickel for doing it."

Tony was confused. "No, it belongs to my . . . uh, father."

"Yeah, well, I got news for you, kid," the man said. "It belongs to me, and I'm not your old man."

Tony reached to stop him from taking the briefcase, but the man snatched it away. "Don't even try it," he said in a mean voice, "or I'll have a cop on you in two seconds flat."

Frantically, Tony looked toward the ticket windows. He waved and started to call for help. But then he saw that nobody was there. The older man had disappeared.

With Tony's money.

Forgetting about the briefcase, Tony looked around the nearly empty station. The man was nowhere in sight. Maybe he just went to another part of the station? Picking up his duffel, Tony ran to the front entrance, searching for a glimpse of the man. But it was too late.

An hour or so later, Tony stood on the Roosevelt Road viaduct, shivering. The wind blowing off Lake Michigan was chilly even on this summer night. He leaned against the concrete railing, looking at the railroad yards to the north. A maze of tracks ran side by side and then forked off in every direction. Lines of boxcars, tanker cars, and passenger cars stood waiting to be hooked onto an engine. By tomorrow, he thought, all of them would be far away. If he went down there and got inside one, so would he.

Beyond the dark railroad yards, farther in the distance, towers ablaze with lights stretched into the sky. Those were the skyscrapers of the Loop, the heart of Chicago. And on the other side of them, though Tony couldn't see it, was home—the apartment above Rocco's Restaurant.

Chicago skyline

Even if he had to walk, Tony could be there by the time the sun came up.

Which was it going to be? Tony was trying to decide when he heard a noise from beneath the viaduct. He peered over the side and saw a thick-waisted man wearing dark clothes and a cap.

The man saw him, too. Tony jerked his head back out of sight.

"Hey!" the man called. "Hey! Somebody up there? Gimme a hand, will ya?"

Hesitantly, Tony peeped into the darkness below. "I haven't got any money," he said, hoping that would discourage the man.

"Yeah? Well, that makes twenty million of us," the man retorted. He seemed to find this funny, for it was followed by a sound that was part cough, part laugh.

"Tell ya what I do have, though," the man said. "I got a nice box of oranges, and if you help me lift them into a boxcar, I'll give you a couple."

Tony looked closer. There was a wooden box at the man's feet, along with another bundle wrapped in a dirty gray cloth. "Where did you get the oranges?" Tony asked.

"I picked 'em off a tree in Florida, sonny," the man said. "What'd you think? You want some or not?"

Tony was curious, and anyway he had no more money for anyone to steal. He made his way to the end of the viaduct and slid down a cinder-covered slope to the tracks below.

"Keep it quiet," hissed the man. "There's bulls patrolling the yards."

Tony looked around. "Bulls? Don't they keep them penned up at the stockyards?"

"Cops, dummy," the man said. "Railroad cops. How long you been ridin' the rails?"

"I never got started," Tony admitted. "Somebody stole my money."

"Your money? How much?"

"Fifteen dollars."

The man laughed again, more like a bark than a laugh. "Well, you can bet on one thing, sonny," he said. "It wasn't bankers who stole your money. They don't bother with small potatoes like that. They only steal big."

Tony looked at him. "Did bankers steal from you?"

The peculiar coughing laugh again. "No, sonny. I was a banker until one day everybody decided to take their money out of the bank. And there wasn't enough. Anyway, no time for any more sad stories. Where were you heading before your money got stolen?"

"California."

"Well, give me a hand with this box. The next train headed west is forming up right over there."

It was a struggle, but they lifted the box of oranges into an empty boxcar. The man boosted himself up and then reached down. "Hand me your duffel," he said.

Tony hesitated. After losing his money, he couldn't afford to lose his clothes.

"Come on," the man said. "The train's not even moving yet. Wait till you try to catch one that's pulling out of the yards while you're carrying a couple of live chickens and a hot apple pie."

The man thought that was the funniest thing of all.

FIVE

A Visitor from America

JULY 30, 1936

DAVID WASN'T ALLOWED TO HAVE THE RADIO ON when Adolf Hitler was giving a speech. His parents hated Hitler, of course. And they thought it was bad for David to listen to him.

But David had already heard all the insults at school. The first time, it had been puzzling to him. Klaus Schichter, one of David's best friends, called him a dirty Jew.

David could hardly believe his ears. At that moment, he began to understand for the first time what had been happening to Germany. Up till then, he knew, yes, he was a Jew. At least his mother was, so that made him a Jew. But it was the same way he was an American, because his father, Jack Aldrich, was an American. David had never really thought of himself as a Jew or an American—he thought of himself as a German. He had been born in Germany and in his twelve years of life had never lived anywhere else.

Yet Germany, it seemed, had suddenly decided that Jews weren't the same as other Germans. Hitler's angry, shouted speeches were broadcast on the radio almost every day. The few times that David had heard them—in a shop, in school when the principal made everyone listen—he was frightened. Not for himself, because that was before he thought of himself as a Jew. No, he was frightened because of the ferocious, unthinking hatred that came pouring out of the radio. It seemed like something too dangerous to have in the room. Like the time when a mad dog had wandered onto their street and Wachtmeister Langen had to come from the police station and shoot him.

With Hitler, it was if a mad dog had gotten loose and people began to praise its madness. One day at school, the principal appeared and took David and two other boys out of the classroom. He led them to another room, where there were children from different grades. All of them were Jewish, and the principal said that from now on they would come to this room for their lessons. Their teacher was the only Jew on the faculty. But he soon left, and now Dame Kindelhoff came in the morning to give them work to do. She didn't really teach. All day she would sit at the teacher's desk and scold people if they spoke or even moved in a way she didn't like. She complained loudly how hard a job it was having to teach Jews.

Pretty soon, Dame Kindelhoff might not have to. One by one, the Jewish students stopped coming to school. It was too much to bear. The taunts of the other students grew louder and nastier each day. Walking to school became a trial as well. Even grown-ups seemed to know which children were Jewish, and they made faces at them or roughly pushed them off the sidewalk as they passed.

David

David hadn't told his parents any of this because he didn't want them to worry. Even though school was no longer as much fun as it had been, David wanted to continue to go there. He liked learning things. Both his parents were scientists, and he wanted to become one too.

Papa and Mama spent most of their time at the Institute for Physical Sciences. At home a cook and two maids took care of David and his sister Esther. Esther was only three, so she wasn't very interesting to talk to. David thought going to school was worth dodging a few stones or ignoring rude chants. He kept hoping that one day everyone would wake up and realize Hitler was crazy—a mad dog. And then everything could go back to being the way it was before.

One day, David's parents came home early from the Institute. That was unusual enough, but they had another surprise. "Put on your good suit and comb your hair, David," Mama said. "We're having a visitor—your father's cousin from America."

"A cousin?" he said, looking up eagerly from his textbook. "Is it the one who has been in the movies?" David's father had so many relatives that it was hard to keep them all straight. Papa didn't talk much about them. David was nine before he learned that the race driver Harry Aldrich was Papa's brother. And it was a year later that David went to see Uncle Harry in a movie. That was when David had decided to concentrate harder on learning English, for the day when he might visit some relatives in the United States.

"She is here for the Olympics," Mama said.

"An athlete?" asked David.

"*Nein*, a trainer, a coach."

David practiced his English phrases all afternoon: "How do you do? I am pleased to meet you. Are you enjoying your stay?"

When the doorbell rang, he ran downstairs to be the first to answer it. Usually one of the maids

Hitler youth

"You hokey-dokey?" she asked.

"I am **David**," he answered. "I am pleased to meet you."

She gave him an odd look. "What should I do with this yegg?"

David brushed some mud from the corner of his eye. "I think you must . . ." He tried to think of the right English word. ". . . release him."

"Yeah?" She sounded disappointed. "Shouldn't we at least call the police?"

David shook his head sadly. "That's Fritzie Langen. His father *is* the police, at least in our district here."

greeted callers and then announced them to the family.

He opened the door, a welcoming phrase on his lips.

And then a hail of brown balls struck him. I was so unexpected that he didn't realize what wa happening. Not until one of them splattere against his cheek. It was a mudball—no, more tha mud—mixed with horse manure from the stab down the street.

A chorus of laughter and cries of, "Look at dirty Jew," told him who had thrown the mudba Boys from school, who used to be his frier Tears of rage came to his eyes and he started shut the door.

But then he heard a loud voice, speaking I lish. "Hey! You kids! What are you tryin pull?" A tall, blonde, muscular woman—loo just like she had stepped from an Olympic G poster—charged up the sidewalk.

The boys took a look at this sudden ap ance of a goddess, and scattered. One, unl than the rest, was caught. Holding the collar Hitler Youth uniform, the goddess held him ground. He wriggled there like a fish.

The goddess turned to David, standin spattered and awed in the doorway. "He called again. David thought that "hey" mu shortened form of "hello."

She frowned, and then flicked Fritzie onto the cobblestones as if he were something foul she had picked up by mistake. "Don't let me catch you around here again, kid," she called.

David didn't know if Fritzie understood English, but he scrambled to his feet and ran as if the Furies were pursuing him.

"So," the woman said, "you're David. I'm your father's cousin Molly Aldrich Woods." She held out her hand.

"I am pleased to meet you," he said again. Her hand, taking his, had so strong a grip that he almost cried out.

Later, after David got cleaned up, he joined the conversation in the parlor. Father was telling Cousin Molly: "It's getting worse every day. I never thought it would be so bad for all of us. Einstein was right to leave Germany when he did. But because I am not Jewish, I thought they would leave my family alone."

"Why don't you pack up and leave right now?" Molly asked.

David's parents looked at each other. "It's not so easy as you think," Father said. "I could leave at any time, because I am an American citizen. The children could go too, because I can get American passports for them. Even Sara could go," he said, squeezing Mother's hand. "But we have decided we cannot leave her parents behind. They are old, and in Germany today they would have a very hard time without us."

"Even though I am a Jew," Mother said, "the government still lets me teach and do research at the Institute. Many Jews have been forbidden to do such work. But the Nazis think the work I do is valuable. Because of that, I can make sure my parents are safe."

Molly shrugged. "Bring them to the United States as well."

Father shook his head. "Many, many people have applied for visas to enter the United States. But only a few are being given."

Noticing that David was listening intently, Mother changed the subject. "That's enough about us," she said. "Tell us about the Olympics. Here, the newspapers all say the Germans will win every event."

Molly laughed. "I doubt that. Our women's track team has some good prospects. I'm eager to see how they do. The first heats aren't until Sunday. Opening ceremonies will take all day Saturday. You know, I can get tickets if you want them."

"Oh, there is no time for us to go," Mother said.

"How about you?" Molly said, looking at David. "Would you like to see the Olympics?"

"Oh, yes," he blurted out. For months the newspapers had been full of stories about the upcoming games. "They say it's going to be a wonderful spectacle."

Father snorted. "Hitler is trying to make the Olympics into a propaganda event for his Nazi regime."

"Really? said Molly. "Well, maybe we can upset his applecart."

David laughed. The adults looked at him, and his face grew red. "I'm sorry," he said. "It's just that the way you speak English is so different from the way we learned in school."

"Is that so?" said Molly. "I guess they don't teach you American English. Stick around and you'll pick it up. So, will you be ready at eight Saturday morning?"

David's parents frowned. "Oh, please, Mother, Father," he said. "I'd love to go."

"I'll get him a pass that will show he's an American," Molly told them. "He can come on the field with our team."

"That I would approve of," Father said.

David's heart leaped.

SIX

Riding the Rails

THE MAN WITH THE STOLEN CRATE OF ORANGES was named Walt. "That's all the name you need out here on the rails, sonny," he told Tony. "It's not polite to ask for last names. Because somebody might be on the run from the law, or have a family somewhere, or escaped from someplace they don't want to go back to."

Tony looked cautiously around the railroad car. In the shadows he could see small groups of huddled figures. The thought that everybody was a criminal or escaped convict of some kind frightened him.

"'Course," Walt went on, "a lot of 'em ain't got no place to go back to. They's just movin' from one place to another, looking for a job or a handout."

Suddenly a man sat down next to them. Tony jumped because the man hadn't made a sound. "Hey, Walt," he said, "you old chicken thief. What'd you get your hooks into this time?"

"I'm just explaining the rules of the road to this young lad," Walt said with as much dignity as he could. He turned to Tony and explained, "This is Philadelphia Phil. You got to be careful of such as him when you're travelin' the rails."

Philadelphia Phil gave a nasty laugh. "I'm not talkin' about this boy," he said. He reached over and tapped the wooden crate that Walt had under his legs.

"Oh, that," said Walt. "That's nothin'. That's just a box of old clothes somebody tossed out."

"I wonder," Phil said, "if you told this boy the rule that if somebody's got more food than they can eat, it's not polite to hide it from the others that are travelin' with them."

"I never done that," said Walt.

Phil sniffed loudly. He looked at Tony. "You smell what I do?" he asked.

Tony took a deep breath and immediately wished he hadn't. Most of what he smelled was a mix of people who hadn't taken a bath in a long time and the cattle that had come to Chicago in this railroad car.

But Philadelphia Phil evidently had a keener sense of smell. "It's oranges," he said. In the darkness, Tony heard a click. His eyes opened wide as he saw the blade of a jackknife in Phil's hand. "I got something here I could peel those oranges with," he told Walt. "In case their skins is too tough."

Grumbling, Walt reached under his legs and pried open the box. "No call for that," he said. "I was gonna give you some. Just thought I'd save it for the trip, is all. Later on, when you're hungry and all these oranges is gone, don't complain to me."

In a little while, six of the oranges were gone. Walt, Phil, and Tony each had eaten two. As far as Tony could tell, that still left pretty many oranges in the crate. Walt shoved it into a dark corner and went to sleep.

He didn't awaken even when the car jolted backward with a loud clang. Tony showed his alarm, but Phil said, "Settle down. That's just the locomotive hooking us up. We'll be out of Chicago before the sun's up."

"How long till we get to California?" Tony asked.

Phil chuckled. "Is that where you're headed? Why, the truth is, this here car might *never* get to California." Seeing the look on Tony's face, he said, "Oh, it's going west, sure enough. But it might only go as far as St. Louis or Omaha before it's loaded up with cargo again. That's when we get off, unless you want to share your bunk with a few dozen cows."

"I thought—Walt said . . ." Tony stammered.

"You can't listen to people like Walt," said Phil. "I guess he told you he used to be somebody important."

"A banker," Tony told him.

"Now, think about it . . . you ever hear a banker talk like him? He talks like a 'bo—a hobo, a bum—one who's been on the road a long time."

Tony had to admit this was true. "So why does he say he was a banker?"

"Why, sonny, you don't know nothing about folks, do you? This your first time on the rails?"

Tony was annoyed that everybody thought he was a greenhorn. "I would have been able to catch a *real* train," he said, "except somebody stole my money."

Phil laughed. "A real train, eh?" he said. "How did your money come to be stolen? Walt didn't take it, did he?"

Tony told Phil the story of how he lost his money.

Phil nodded. "That's an easy scam," he said. "You know what? The second man, the one who picked up the briefcase—he was in on it too. His job was to grab your attention while the first man got away."

Surprised, Tony thought it over. "How did you know that?" he asked.

"Never you mind," said Phil. "But don't worry about it. There's lots of ways to lose your money. Most of the people in this car have lost more than you did. Some of them lost everything they worked for over a lifetime."

Tony sat with his legs dangling out the open door of the car, which was picking up speed. "How'd they do that?" he asked.

"Lots of ways. Banks foreclosed on their farms or businesses. They lost their jobs and couldn't keep up the payments on their houses. They got too deep in debt, and somebody came and took everything they had."

"It doesn't seem right," said Tony. He thought about his parents and wondered if there was any chance they would lose the restaurant.

"It *isn't* right," Philadelphia Phil said. "But that's why Walt pretends he used to be a banker. He wants to think he was important. Most folks do. It sort of makes up for the fact that they aren't anything now."

The train went around a curve, and Tony had to catch hold of the door to keep his balance. He looked back and caught a last glimpse of the high towers in the midst of the city. They were far off now and getting farther away every second. He wondered if he would ever see them again, and turned away so Philadelphia Phil wouldn't see him cry.

Tony slept a long time, even though the floor had nothing but a layer of straw on it. It was hunger that woke him up. For a second before he opened his eyes, he was ready to sit down to a big breakfast downstairs in the restaurant.

Then the car bounced over a rough part in the rails, and he remembered where he was. He crawled over to where Walt was sitting. "Can I have another orange?" he asked.

Walt pointed to the box, which was empty of everything but a few peels. "The fellas cleaned me out," he said. "You gotta sleep lighter than you do if you want to catch your share. Somebody got off when the train stopped for water last night and snagged a few loaves of bread from a bakery trash barrel. But that's all gone too."

Tony's stomach turned over. By now the sun was high in the sky and the inside of the railroad car was hot, even though the door was open. "Isn't there any water?" Tony asked.

Walt took from his cloth bag a small glass bottle sealed with a cork. He held it up to the light and shook it. Tony could see about an inch of water in the bottom.

"First off, you ought to find some bottle of your own to carry," said Walt. "But since you don't, you can take a sip of this. We're due to stop in another hour or so, and I can refill it then."

Tony took the bottle and looked at the brownish water inside. Flecks of something white were floating in it. But he was too thirsty to refuse. He closed his eyes, put the bottle to his lips, and tilted his head back.

It was warm, but didn't taste as bad as he feared. When he lowered the bottle, it was empty. Walt snatched it back. "Hmph!" he said. "You could leave a little for somebody else."

Fortunately the train started to slow down not long afterward. The other men and boys in the boxcar stood up and gathered near the doorway. When the train ground to a halt, they jumped out.

On this side of the train stood a large wooden water tank. As Tony watched, the train crew stepped down from the engine and began to pull the spout of the tank down.

Suddenly Tony realized he was all alone. A hand reached from under the train and pulled on his ankle. "Come on, dummy," hissed Walt. "If they see you, they'll come down and close the car door."

Tony bent over and slid underneath the train. On the other side was a small railroad station. Beyond that, a few houses and stores. The men who had been in the boxcar had already lined up at the public drinking fountain outside the station. Tony saw a few headed for the town.

"How long will the train stop?" Tony asked Walt.

"Half an hour or so," said Walt. "Maybe more if the crew decides to eat here."

Some of the men in the boxcar had a little money, and they went into the lunch counter in the station. Tony felt even more angry at himself for losing his money. He could have bought a hot dog for a nickel or a bowl of soup for a dime.

Walt slapped him on the back. "Let's see if we can rustle some grub, sonny," he said. Tony followed as Walt started down a dusty little street. "You're not going to steal anything, are you?" Tony asked.

"No, but we might find something that's been lost," Walt said.

The houses were all in need of a coat of paint, and the small yards weren't much more than crabgrass and weeds. But there were signs of life. A clothesline draped with fresh laundry stretched across a side yard. Somebody had been working on a Model T Ford in the front yard of another house.

Without warning, Walt stopped and grabbed Tony's arm. "See this house? The one with curtains in the front windows?"

Tony nodded. "Go on up and knock on the front door," Walt said. "Tell the woman you're willing to work for food."

"Why this house?" Tony asked.

Walt pointed to some symbols drawn in chalk on the wooden fence in front of the house. "Somebody before us got a handout here. They left that X mark. If they got chased away, they woulda left three slanted lines."

OK, all right   *This place is not safe*   *Kind woman lives here; tell pitiful story*

"But what if she gives me a lot of work to do?" Tony asked. "I'll miss the train."

"Listen, sonny," Walt said, "first off, if you miss one train, you can catch another. What good is it gonna do you to catch the train if you're starvin'?"

Walt gave Tony a little push to encourage him. "Besides, the lady and the triangle drawing means she'll probably feel sorry for ya if you give her a good story. Being a kid is a big advantage, believe me."

Tony didn't feel like it was. As he walked slowly up the front steps of the porch, he felt ashamed. But his empty stomach rumbled, and he knocked on the door.

When it opened, a young woman stood there, holding a baby in one arm. Her brown hair was up in a bun, but strands of it fell down on her face. She looked like she'd been working.

Tony stammered, trying to remember what Walt had told him.

"What do you want?" she asked. She had a nice voice, but sounded impatient.

"Um, I wonder if I could trade some food for some work," Tony said. "I mean . . . work for food."

She smiled a little. "I guess you're hungry," she said.

"Yes, ma'am," said Tony. He could feel his face get red.

"Seems like lots of hungry folks come by here lately," she added.

Guiltily, Tony wondered if he should tell her about the marks on her fence.

"I've got some pie left over from last night's supper," she said. "But I haven't got any work for you to do."

Tony looked around. Something at the corner of the house caught his eye. "Those are tomato plants, aren't they?" he asked.

"Yes, I put some in, along with beans and summer squash. They never seem to do very well for me, though."

"They need to be weeded and staked up," Tony told her. "My grandfather showed me how when I was younger. I could do that for you, if you wanted."

"Well, I guess that'd be fair," she said.

It turned out that she had a hoe, so that made the job easier. Tony snapped some branches off a dead tree to make stakes, and the woman let him tear up an old rag to tie the plants to the stakes.

By the time he finished, she was standing and watching. "You sure did a neat job of that," she said. "But do you think it'll help the plants?"

"Yes, ma'am. You've always got to keep the weeds out. Tomato roots are close to the surface so weeds take water from them. And if you stake the plants you're less likely to get diseases or rot."

"Well, that's worth a couple pieces of pie," she said. Tony heard the train whistle. "Would you like to come in for a glass of lemonade too?" the woman asked.

He was torn. "Um, no thanks. If I could just have the pie, that'd be fine." Looking as if her feelings were hurt, she handed him a package wrapped with wax paper. He turned abruptly and ran.

As he reached the fence, he looked over his shoulder and yelled, "Better wash this chalk off, ma'am!" He didn't know if she'd understood him.

The train was starting to move by the time he reached the station. Tony realized he was on the wrong side of it. The open door to the boxcar faced the other side of the tracks, and there was no way for him to get there now.

Then he saw a couple of men grab hold of ladders on the sides of the cars. It was worth a try, but the train was slowly picking up speed. He reached out with one hand, still holding the pie with the other. His hand caught a metal rung, but slipped off.

The train started to pull away from him. He ran faster, and another car pulled alongside. Desperately, he grabbed for the ladder and caught hold of it.

A stab of pain shot down his fingers and wrist as the train pulled him right off his feet. He heard the heavy metal wheels clicking just below, and realized that if he fell now he would be crushed beneath the train. He stuffed a corner of the wax paper package into his mouth. Now he could use both hands to lift himself, but it was still tough to get up the ladder.

Finally, he reached the top and swung over the side. He lay on the wooden roof of the car, breathing heavily. After a minute, he sat up, cradling the precious pie in his hands. He'd never felt so hungry.

He unwrapped the package and took a greedy bite. It tasted good—almost anything would have— but strange. Working in the restaurant, he'd learned enough about food to recognize the taste of most things. But this? Apple pie? Peach?

He took another bite, chewing more slowly. It was sweet and salty at the same time. Curious, he lifted the crust to look. Then he realized that most of the filling of the pie was Ritz crackers.

It made him upset for a second, and then he realized what that meant. The woman herself was so poor, she couldn't afford to buy real fruit to make her family a pie. And yet she had shared it with a stranger. He looked back at the town, which was so small that it already seemed like a toy village.

SEVEN

Opening Day

AUGUST 1, 1936

ON SATURDAY, THE DAY THE OLYMPICS WERE scheduled to begin, a black Daimler car with American flags flying from the fenders stopped in front of the Aldrich house.

David had been awake for hours. At school, the non-Jewish students had been invited to take part in the opening ceremonies. He wondered what they would think if they saw him with the American team.

A chauffeur was driving the Daimler limousine. David had expected he would be the only one in the car, because Cousin Molly was staying with the American team at the Olympic Village.

69

She said she would see him at the stadium.

However, the back door opened after the car stopped, and an elderly gentleman got out. He had a lively step and a bright look in his eye that made him seem youthful despite his gray hair.

"*Guten Tag,*" he said with an American accent. "You must be David."

"How do you do," David replied, shaking the man's hand.

"I'm your father's Uncle Georgie," he said. "I just arrived last night, and Molly said I should ride along with you to the stadium."

David tried to remember anything his father had said about Uncle Georgie. "Are you in the movies?" he asked.

Uncle Georgie chuckled. "No, I'm not one of the on-stage Aldriches," he said. "My parents put me in a play when I was an infant, thinking I'd follow the family tradition. Instead, I threw up on the heroine. It was a good thing, really. Not for her—but for me, because I stayed backstage after that and learned how things worked. That made me an inventor."

Georgie

"Oh!" said David. "What have you invented?" He got into the car, and it glided down the street. During the night, workers had put up fresh Nazi banners on every other streetlight. The black swastika against a blood-colored background cast a chill through David. Far off, he could hear the sound of thousands of singing voices.

Uncle Georgie was still talking. "I gave your father his introduction to science. I let him and your uncle Harry use my Oldsmobile in a race. I showed your father how to improve the car's engine so they could."

"That sounds like fun," said David. "And did they win the race?"

"Well . . . we beat the other automobile," recalled Uncle Georgie. "There was a girl, my niece Peggy, who rode a horse ahead of them. But it was muddy that day, so she was cheating really. It wasn't a true test."

David hadn't heard this story. He'd have to ask Father about it. "Have you come to Germany because of science?" he asked Uncle Georgie. "Or just to see the Olympics?"

"A little of both, really. I've been working on the idea of television—pictures that will be broadcast like radio programs. Several scientists have produced television receivers, but none is completely successful. The Germans have announced they will broadcast television pictures of the Olympic Games. That was quite a shock to me. Seeing is believing though, so I came over for a look."

As their car drew nearer to the Reich Sports Field—the immense stadium that had been built for the Olympics—the driver had to slow down. The streets were clogged with people who had turned out for the festivities. Policemen were checking the passes of all cars.

Finally, the driver turned to David and Uncle Georgie and said, "I'm sorry I cannot take you any closer. Only official cars can drive down Unter den Linden today."

"That's all right," said Uncle Georgie. "We can walk the rest of the way."

Stepping from the car into the crowd was a shock, however. The waves of sound made David wish he'd stayed home. Bands played the German national anthem and Nazi marching songs. Thousands of people sang along. Soldiers were everywhere, looking menacing in their crisp brown uniforms. Special SS troops could be identified by their Nazi armbands. Marching crowds of boys and girls in Hitler Youth uniforms, carrying banners and flags, added to the din with their chanting and cheers.

It was almost impossible to get through the crowd. "We might as well stand here and watch," said Uncle Georgie. He squeezed into a spot next to one of the linden trees that lined the wide avenue. An SS officer gave them a look, and David cringed. Although David looked nothing like the ugly cartoons of Jews that Nazis posted around the city, he felt as if the SS man could somehow tell he was Jewish.

But Uncle Georgie held up a stadium pass with the American flag on it. The SS officer's frown turned into a smile. "*Wilkommen*," he said. He moved on down the line of people standing at the curb.

"Molly warned me to avoid the police," remarked Uncle Georgie. "But that one was certainly polite."

David bit his tongue. He knew that for weeks the message had been blaring over the radio: "Be respectful of Olympic guests, even if you suspect they are Jewish."

"Look at that," someone behind them shouted, pointing at the sky. A cheer went up from the crowd as the giant airship *Hindenburg* floated into sight. Filled with hydrogen, it was an aluminum frame covered by a silver linen bag. The tail fins of this mighty zeppelin airship were emblazoned with swastikas, the red and black Nazi symbol.

"Magnificent," said Uncle Georgie. "I believe lighter-than-air travel is the wave of the future–not airplanes. And Germany is leading the way in developing its zeppelin airships."

"Airplanes are faster than zeppelins," David pointed out.

the Hindenburg

Uncle Georgie waved his hand. "That's only a small detail," he said. "The zeppelins can carry far heavier loads, and their safety record is better than airplanes."

Just then, the crowd's cheering became even louder. David looked up the avenue to where the marble arch called the Brandenburg Gate stood. Up there, people were shrieking and thousands of arms were raised in the Nazi salute. He could see a black Mercedes-Benz with the top down. Standing in the front seat was a man dressed in a military uniform. The bill of the cap shaded his eyes, but it was clear who he was. Even if David could not see him, he would have known by the cries of "Heil Hitler" that roared from the vast throng of people who were lined along the avenue.

The upraised arms rippled down the street, following the car. All around David, people were lifting their arms in tribute. He felt their excitement, but forced himself to keep his arms at his side. He had promised Mother that never, never would he give the salute.

As the car went by, Hitler turned his head in David's direction. For an instant, it seemed as if his bright blue eyes were pointed directly at the spot where he stood. A thrill of fear went through David's body, as he realized that his refusal to salute had been noticed.

Then the parade of cars moved on, carrying with it the cheers and marching music. People turned to follow it toward the stadium.

Weakly, David put his hand against the tree to steady himself. "Are you all right?" asked Uncle Georgie.

"Yes, I am just . . . fine." David tried to remember the word Molly had used. It was a funny word, and he wanted to say it now. "Hokeydokey." He felt better after he had remembered.

"Well, come on then. We have reserved seats but it will be hard to get through this crowd anyway."

It did take them nearly an hour before they were settled. They were sitting in a section with many Americans, so David felt somewhat safe.

He had never been in a stadium so large. It seemed as if it could hold everyone in Berlin. The newspapers had said it had seats for 100,000 people. In the center of the stadium was a huge grass-covered field, cut so perfectly that each blade of grass seemed to stand at attention. Surrounding it was a cinder track, colored a startling shade of red, where the races would be run.

The Olympic teams began to march in formation from a tunnel at the opposite end of the stadium. The crowd, in a joyous mood, applauded each nation's athletes.

Uncle Georgie suddenly grasped David's arm. "There!" he shouted. "There it is!"

David strained his eyes in the direction Georgie was pointing. He had no idea what might have excited the older man so much. David had been waiting for the American team to appear, but since the country's name, '*Vereinigte Staaten Nordamerikas*', was near the end of the alphabet, the team hadn't appeared yet.

"It's the camera," Uncle Georgie said. "That's the German television camera." Now David saw it, a big, black, ugly machine. Even though it was on wheels, it took three men to move it, and another to carry the thick cable that ran behind.

"I've got to see it," cried Georgie. And with that he bounded out of his seat and started down the concrete steps.

Without thinking, David ran after him. He felt he ought to warn Uncle Georgie not to go onto the field. Things were different here in Germany than they were in the United States. Even David's father had expressed his disapproval of the lack of order and discipline Americans displayed.

But Uncle Georgie was too fast. Before David could catch up to him, he had reached the bottom of the steps. Hopping over the wall and onto the running track, he stopped and turned.

"Hurry up," Uncle Georgie called to David. "This is going to be very interesting."

"You can't–" David began. But Uncle Georgie reached up, grabbed his hand, and virtually pulled him onto the field.

Just then, the crowd stood and cheered. David was startled. Then he saw that the Italian team–Italy and Germany were strong allies–had just appeared at the mouth of the tunnel.

Fortunately, this meant that no one noticed Uncle Georgie and David, who were running through the neat lines of athletes, all clad in the bright colors of their countries' flags.

David looked around, bewildered and awed. He nearly collided with a Greek athlete who was carrying the team banner. He called an apology over his shoulder, hurrying onward. For it was even more important not to lose sight of Uncle Georgie.

Finally, they came to an open space in the grassy playing field. A long corridor had been left open between the assembled teams. Right in the middle stood a small platform with a microphone on it. Pointed at the platform was the large black box that had excited Uncle Georgie . . .

. . . who was at this very moment–David saw with horror–headed toward the platform as if he belonged there.

And as if that weren't bad enough, from the other direction came a knot of people. Striding in front was the man who obviously did belong on the platform: Hitler himself.

E I G H T

A Free Meal

AUGUST 2, 1936

TONY WAS RUNNING ACROSS THE TOPS OF THE railroad cars, jumping from one to another. It wasn't difficult as long as the train wasn't moving. But he wondered what he was going to do when he came to the last car.

Earlier that morning, Walt had awakened him as the train pulled into the railroad yard. "This is St. Louis," Walt told Tony. "Probably have to find a new train here, if you want to keep goin' west."

"Aren't you?" Tony asked.

"Nah, I wanna stop and find a cheap hotel room. Sleep in a bed for a few days. My back's been bothering me."

"But you don't have any money."

"I can panhandle, or go pearl divin'. I'll find a way to scrape up fifty cents or a buck a day."

"Pearl diving?"

Walt smiled. "Wash dishes, sonny."

"Oh." Tony thought of all the dishes he'd washed in the restaurant. He didn't run away just so he could do that again.

"Well, thanks for the oranges," Tony said. "And for showing me . . . you know."

"Yeah," Walt said, shaking Tony's hand. "I'll see you again, sonny. You know, you ride the rails long enough, you run into the same people over and over. Me and Philadelphia Phil might as well have a string tied to each other. That's how often our paths cross."

"Well," said Tony, "I don't plan on riding the rails any longer than it takes to get to California."

Walt nodded. "Yeah, lots of folks say that. They think California's just sitting there with loads of work for people to do. Fruit hangin' from the trees waitin' to be picked. Weather so fine you can just lie down by a stream at night and count the stars. Take a look around you, sonny. Notice that there's just as many people ridin' the rails *away* from California as there is goin' *to* California."

Tony thought about that, but before he could reply, Walt turned and started across the dark railroad yards. "How do you tell which cars are going east and which are going west?" Tony called after him.

A wind blew across the yards, raising a cloud of black dust. Tony didn't quite hear Walt's answer. But he thought it sounded like, "Don't much matter."

Well, it did matter to Tony. He wished Philadelphia Phil was around, but they'd lost him sometime before the train crossed the Mississippi River.

Tony looked around, feeling alone. He saw a car marked, "Santa Fe Railroad." He wasn't sure, but when he'd been paying attention in geography class, he thought the teacher said Santa Fe was out west someplace.

Trouble was, the door to the car was locked. By now, however, Tony had learned that most boxcars had a trapdoor on top. If you climbed up the ladder on the side of the car, you could get in that way.

As it turned out, the trapdoor on this car was locked too. Tony sat down on top, wondering what to do. It was probably safer here than wandering through the yards. Walt and the other 'bos warned him that the railroad police in St. Louis were particularly mean. "They'll beat you up for no other reason than the exercise," Walt had said.

So Tony decided to sit up here and wait for the car to be hooked to a train. After that, he could look for an unlocked car. Anyway, as long as it didn't rain, riding on top of the cars was supposed to be better than inside. "Till you come to a tunnel," Phil had cautioned him. "Then you climb down between the cars and hold on for dear life. Personally I'd rather ride inside than on top. But you sure see a lot from up there."

Right now, there wasn't much to see. Just a few lights in the dirty windows of the old railroad terminal. St. Louis wasn't as bright a city as Chicago. Tony felt a pang of homesickness, but he shook it off. St. Louis must be at least halfway to California. He'd reach Hollywood soon.

His body tensed when he heard the sound of a locomotive slowly chugging this way. When the clang of metal came, he was ready. One by one, the locomotive picked up other cars. Pretty soon it would have a full train, head out of the yards and go west. He hoped.

Then Tony noticed part of the sky getting pink. All right, he told himself. That's the sunrise. Which direction was that? East? He was pretty sure it was. So that must mean west was the opposite direction. He closed his eyes and imagined a map. He stuck one arm out toward the east . . .

"Hey, you!" Tony's eyes snapped open. The light was still dim, but it was bright enough for him to see the guard on the ground next to the car.

"Get down from there!" the man called. Philadelphia Phil had told Tony never to obey such an order. "They get you down on the ground, they'll just hammer your head," he said. "Stay up high and if they come after you, run."

When Tony didn't climb down, that's just what happened. The guard scaled the ladder to the top of the car. Tony could see the ugly-looking club he carried. He didn't need any urging to run away.

The man was slow and Tony had no trouble outdistancing him. But then the train began to move. The first jolt nearly knocked Tony off his feet. But he recovered and took a quick look back. The guard was used to running on a moving train, and was a little closer now. Besides, carrying his duffel bag slowed Tony down.

He ran on, looking frantically for an open trapdoor in one of the cars. Then he heard another angry shout. As he looked up, he saw a second guard coming toward him from the other direction.

There was nothing else to do. "If you gotta jump," Phil had told him, "run with the train. You're less likely to break your legs."

Tony took a deep breath and leaped, hoping that the ground below him would be soft. His legs kept running furiously while he was still in the air.

The next thing he knew, he was sliding on rough, sharp cinders. His head struck the ground and he saw flashes of light. Far off, he heard the harsh laughter of the railroad guards.

At least they didn't chase him. After a minute, Tony picked himself up. His legs and arms all moved, but a pain like fire ran down the side of his left leg. When he put his hand there, he touched blood. His pants leg was shredded and his leg had been scraped raw.

It hurt even more when he stood on it, but he figured he'd better keep moving. He'd be helpless if a guard found him now. He saw the lights of automobiles moving off to his right and headed toward them.

By the time the sun came up, the blood on his leg had dried. He had found a truck stop that was open all night. Around to the back of it, he changed into his other pair of pants and a fresh shirt.

Tony still didn't have any money, so he decided to try something else Phil had told him about. Trying to look confident he went inside the truck stop and sat down in a booth.

Fortunately there were three truckers at the counter, buying coffee and chatting with the waitress. She hardly gave Tony a glance as she went over to his booth, setting down a glass of water and a menu.

His mouth watered as he looked a the list of food. Ham and eggs, buttered toast, sausage links, pancakes with maple syrup—he could have anything he wanted. If only he had a quarter. He'd never realized before how important money was.

He knew if the waitress brought him food and he couldn't pay for it, he'd probably have to wash dishes for the rest of the day. For some reason, he didn't want to. He would lose a whole day and be no better off when he finished. And washing dishes was too much like what he'd done at home for as long as he could remember.

So he did what Phil told him. There was a bowl of saltine crackers on the table, along with a bottle of catsup, a glass jar of mustard, and salt and pepper shakers.

He picked up one of the saltines and put catsup on it. Then he covered it with another cracker and popped it into his mouth. It was too big, really, but he was hungry. He glanced at the waitress, who was laughing at something one of the truckers had said. She had a nice laugh.

Quickly, Tony made two, three, four more cracker sandwiches. To vary the flavor, he added mustard to one, but that didn't taste as good. Finally, he just dipped crackers into the glass of water so they'd go down faster.

It didn't take long before he stopped feeling so hungry. He could have used another glass of water, but asking for one would be pushing his luck.

Then he noticed a man sitting at the far end of the room. He was watching Tony, not the waitress. At once, Tony looked away. He stood up and headed for the door. He started to stuff a few more crackers into his pants pocket, but then thought better of it. After all, he told himself, he hadn't stolen anything. The worst they could do was make him wash a few dishes. They couldn't send him to jail or anything.

As he stepped out the door into the parking lot, he tensed himself. But nobody called out, "Stop thief!" or anything else.

Even so, he wanted to get away as fast as he could. He started off down the road. There were more cars on it now, and no sidewalk. So he had to walk in the dusty ditch alongside. The uneven ground didn't make his leg feel any better.

Tony turned and faced the oncoming traffic, holding out his thumb. Maybe he looked too shabby to get a ride, but it was worth a try.

It wasn't any more than a minute before a rusty Ford pickup truck slowed down and stopped. Tony thought he was pretty lucky until he opened the door and saw the driver. It was the man who had watched him in the restaurant.

"Well?" the man said when he saw Tony hesitate. "You need a ride, don't you?"

Tony got in. At least the truck was headed in the right direction. The man threw it into gear and with a shudder and a rattle it began to move. "Saw you in the restaurant back there," the man shouted over the din. "You looked hungry."

Tony shrugged. "Guess so," he said.

The man pulled a pack of cigarettes from his shirt pocket and offered it to Tony. "Wanna smoke?"

"No," Tony said. He hated the smell of tobacco. He had cleaned too many dirty ashtrays in the restaurant.

The man laughed. "Good," he said. "I don't like people who work for me to smoke. Causes fires."

Tony looked at him. "Work for you?"

"You're a big strong fella, looks like," said the man. "Ever work on a farm?"

Tony almost said no. Then he remembered. "My grandfather had a little farm where he grew tomatoes and zucchini and grapes. I helped out there."

"You'll get three meals and a quarter a day less expenses," the man said.

Tony ignored the part about expenses. The thought of three meals plus a quarter was enough. In a couple weeks, he'd have . . . well, enough to get to California, probably.

"What do I have to do?" he asked.

Olympic Victories

AUGUST 1–5, 1936

DAVID BREATHED A SIGH OF RELIEF. UNCLE GEORGIE had walked to the side of the platform to examine the television camera there. Hitler paid no attention to him. He had turned to accept a bouquet of roses brought by a little girl.

Hitler immediately handed them to an underling and stepped onto the platform. He stood stiffly behind a row of microphones as the rest of the Olympic teams filed into the stadium.

David wanted to run back to the stands, but that would only attract attention. He edged toward the platform, trying to blend in with the camera operators. He managed to get next to Uncle

Georgie, and tugged at his sleeve. "Maybe we should get back to our seats," David suggested.

"Hm, oh no, we have field passes," said Georgie. "Didn't I give you one?" He fumbled in his coat pocket and handed David a piece of cardboard with the Olympic rings and the Nazi swastika on it. David's hand was a little sweaty as he took it.

"Look at this," Uncle Georgie said as if he'd found a sack of gold coins on the ground. Instead, he held up one of the thick black cables that ran underneath the platform. "The Germans aren't transmitting television pictures through the air," he explained. "They're only sending them via cables, which has been possible for years. In other words, they haven't developed anything new."

Just then, the crowd gave a terrific roar, drowning out anything else Uncle Georgie might have said. The German team—coming at the end of the Olympic parade—had just entered the stadium.

Even Hitler was applauding as the German athletes—dressed entirely in white uniforms—took their places of honor in front of him. Looking around the stadium, David saw that all the spectators, except a few foreigners, had their arms raised in the Nazi salute. "Sieg . . . Heil . . ." came the chant over and over. It was deafening.

Then Hitler raised his own hand, gesturing for silence. Almost at once, an eerie quiet descended.

Hitler stepped forward and began to speak: "I declare the Games in Berlin . . ." Giant loudspeakers magnified his voice so that it echoed up to the farthest row of seats. ". . . to celebrate the eleventh Olympiad of the modern era . . ."

Then there was silence again. Or nearly so. All the loudspeakers went dead, and only the people on or near the platform could hear Hitler finish the sentence, ". . . as open." He continued, but there was a puzzled murmur from the crowd. David realized that without the microphone, Hitler's power evaporated like dew in the morning sun. He sounded like any other man.

The people next to him realized it too, and began to look for the source of the trouble.

David found it first. With horror, he turned his head and saw Uncle Georgie, smiling. In each hand he held one of the two sections of cord he had just unplugged.

"Put them back together," David whispered, trying not to attract attention.

"It's just as I said," Uncle Georgie replied with a self-satisfied nod.

"That's not the *television*," David told him. "It's the loudspeakers."

Georgie looked around and noticed the commotion on the platform and the sudden silence in the stadium. A couple of people were pointing toward him. He smoothly connected the two cables, and once more Hitler's voice roared out over the crowd.

Fortunately, Uncle Georgie was able to convince Hitler's underlings that he had fixed the problem, not caused it. They were so impressed that they brought him to shake Hitler's hand after the opening ceremony.

Afterward, they met Molly at the Olympic Village. There were no contests on the first day, so all the athletes were leaving to explore the city. Molly introduced David and Georgie to several members of the American team.

One was a young woman who was even taller than Molly herself. "This is Helen Stephens," Molly said. "She already holds the world record in the hundred-meter dash." David found his hand enclosed completely in the woman's. He wondered if all American women were Amazons like these.

"Where is Jesse Owens?" David asked. "The newspapers say he's the best runner America has."

"He's probably the best in the world," Molly replied. "My only worry is that all the interviews he's forced to give will distract him. The German journalists ask him questions that have nothing to do with sport. They think they can make him look like a fool."

"That's not fair," said David.

"Well, Owens is a college student. He can handle himself," said Molly. "It's just that he should have time to concentrate on the events. Running your best is as much a mental feat as it is physical."

That evening, Uncle Georgie came to dinner at the Aldriches' house. Father was glad to see him, but seemed distracted throughout the meal. Over coffee and dessert, he suddenly asked, "How long are you staying in Germany, Georgie?"

"Well, I hoped to see a fuller demonstration of the television apparatus," replied Uncle Georgie.

"I might be able to arrange that," Father told him. "I know the people at the Institute who are in charge of it. But I was hoping you could leave before the Games are over."

"Why?"

"I would like you to take David and his sister Esther to America."

David nearly dropped his ice-cream spoon.

"There are rumors," Father continued, "that after the Olympics Hitler is going to crack down with harsher regulations against Jews. Sara and I have decided to take her parents out of the country as soon as possible. But the children will be safer if they travel with you and Molly."

Uncle Georgie nodded. "We have American passports."

"Yes," Father said. "You can take them out to California and leave them with my brother Harry for now. He has a large estate, and I'm sure he won't mind. I'll send him a telegram before you leave."

Uncle Georgie looked doubtful. "I'm not sure Harry is the most reliable person for taking care of children."

David frowned at that. There was nothing he'd like better than living with his uncle Harry. Maybe he could learn to drive a race car.

Father chuckled and said, "Why, Georgie! You were always the most adventurous person in the family. I hope you're not getting old."

Uncle Georgie shrugged. "I'll be glad to take the children wherever you like. Perhaps we can book passage on the *Hindenburg*. It's going to leave on a transatlantic flight Thursday."

David's head was spinning. He wanted to go to America, but things were happening so fast it seemed like a dream.

The next day, Father took Georgie to the Institute. David still had a pass, so he went to the Games alone. The events were finally starting. First was the men's 100-meter dash. There were too many contestants for one race, so today there would be 12 preliminary races, or heats.

Like David, the crowd was eager to see if Jesse Owens was as fast as they'd heard. They had to wait, for he wasn't scheduled to run until the last heat. Finally, his turn came. He and the other runners used trowels to dig holes behind the starting line. They slipped the tips of their shoes into the holes to get a flying start.

The crowd hushed when Owens and the others bent over. David could hear the starter cry, "*Auf die Plätze . . . Fertig . . .*" and then the explosion of his pistol firing.

What happened next was amazing. In a short race like the 100-meter, the runners are usually separated by less than a meter. But Owens exploded

Jesse Owens

forward and was two or three strides ahead in the first few seconds. By the finish, he was several meters in front of all the other runners.

The crowd couldn't contain itself. People burst into applause and began chanting Owens's name. He acknowledged the cheers with a smile and a wave of his arm. David thought he didn't even look as if he were out of breath.

That evening, David told Father about the American's victory. "Hitler won't like it if Owens does well," said Father. "He thinks of Negroes the same as he does Jews."

That, of course, made David root even harder for the Americans to win. In the next few days, he got his wish. Owens won a gold medal in both the 100-meter and the 200-meter races. He also led the United States to victory in the 400-meter relay race.

The German team captured its share of medals as well. David noticed that Hitler usually appeared in the stadium just before an event that the Germans were expected to win. He was rewarded by seeing German victories in the shot put, hammer throw, and javelin.

The competition between the American and German women was fierce too. But as Molly had predicted, Helen Stephens won the gold in the women's 100 meters. Hitler had given winners from other countries a curt salute from his box. But after Helen Stephens won her race, he sent word that he would like to congratulate her personally.

That evening, David asked Molly what Hitler had said to Helen. "It was the funniest thing," said Molly. "She said he gave her that big Nazi salute of his."

"What did she do?" David asked.

Helen Stephens and Adolf Hitler

"Oh, she told me, 'I just stuck my hand out for a good old Missouri handshake.'"

Molly laughed. "To tell you the truth, I've had enough of these Nazis saluting and marching around like bullies. I hope you're ready to leave. Your father wants us to get you out of here in a hurry.

"I'm ready," David told her.

The final events of the track-and-field competition were held the next day. A feeling of excitement ran through the crowd. In the long jump, Germany had an athlete who might at last defeat the great Jesse Owens.

Luz Long was the champion long jumper of Germany. Schoolboys tried to imitate his graceful jumping style, in which he seemed to float effortlessly through the air with his hands held high over his head.

When Hitler appeared in his seat of honor to view the event, a murmur went through the stadium. It meant that almost certainly Luz Long would win.

Long and Owens soon outjumped all the other athletes. Now each of them had two chances at a final jump. Long went first, drawing cries of awe from the spectators. He reached 7.87 meters, to go into the lead. Then Owens took his place at the starting line. Silence from the crowd as he sailed through

Luz Long

the air, legs kicking, and landed past Long's mark. The announcer's voice came over the loudspeakers: 7.94 meters.

Long lined up for his final effort. Everyone in the stadium rose to their feet. Even Hitler stood, his hands clenched on the railing in front of him. But the pressure was too great, and Long's foot traveled past the foul line before he jumped. False start, the referee ruled.

Owens was now guaranteed the gold medal, but he chose to take his final jump anyway. This time, he soared past all the previous marks. The crowd was stunned when the distance was announced: 8.04 meters. The applause that followed was sincere: Owens had become the first athlete ever to break the 8-meter jump mark.

Once again the American national anthem played as Owens mounted to the top of the medal stand. For David, it was a moment he would never forget. He was overcome with pride. Owens leaned forward so the medal could be slipped around his neck. David didn't even know the words to the American national anthem. But by now he knew the music by heart. And he realized that the song was in his heart as well. He was already starting to feel like an American.

TEN

Escape!

AUGUST 8–9, 1936

TONY WAS EXHAUSTED. HE'D NEVER WORKED SO hard in his life. His fingers were cracked and bleeding, his arms and back were sunburned, and the muscles in his body ached.

Dinner was nothing but a scoop of lima beans, grits, and a few flecks of what might be meat. Tony didn't let himself think about that. He was too hungry.

Really, he had hardly let himself think about anything in the last seven days. The man who had picked him up was named Schiner. He owned a farm, and when he needed people to work on it, all he had to do was drive down to the highway.

Tony slept—and ate and worked—with half a dozen other boys. Schiner had found them the same way he found Tony. None of them was very old. In fact, two of the boys were younger than Tony.

One of them explained why. "If you're seventeen, you can get into one of the CCC camps that President Roosevelt set up. They make you work hard too, but at least they treat you decent. So people say. They pay a dollar a day and give you three squares—real food, not this mush. Schiner feeds us the same reason he feeds horses—just so we'll keep workin' the next day."

Right now, the work was mostly picking corn. It wasn't even the kind of corn you could eat, sweet and tender, like the silver corn Mom served when it was in season. This was tough yellow corn that was turned into food for pigs and cattle. Besides picking the ears of corn, the boys on Schiner's farm had to slop the pigs, milk cows, and hoe the weeds in the fields. It was hard work, but each day that went by, Tony mentally added another quarter to the stack he hoped to have when he left.

Until one day, Eddie, the oldest of the boys, just disappeared. It was strange because he'd left his clothes in the bunkroom where the boys slept. Ron, who slept in the bunk next to his, said Eddie was planning to ask for his money and leave.

"He figured he had enough of this," Ron told the others. "But I don't believe he'd leave all his things behind. Look at this," he said. He opened the cardboard suitcase under Eddie's bed. Inside was a framed photograph of a girl. Ron read what was written across it: "I'll wait for you forever—Annie."

"That's from his girlfriend," Ron said. "He showed it to me once. Said he was going to make good and go back home to marry her someday. He'd never leave without taking that, believe me."

"Not unless he was driven off," said Jake, a short, wiry boy whose face looked thin and pinched. "I heard some arguing last night. Eddie and Schiner were yelling at each other up at the main house. I couldn't tell what they were saying, except that Schiner didn't want to pay Eddie what he thought he had earned. Schiner kept talking about expenses."

"He said that to me too," Tony remembered. "What does that mean?"

Luke shrugged. "I grew up in West Virginia," he said. "My pa was a coal miner. The mine owners run the whole town. Had what they call a company store, where you had to buy food and other stuff. We paid rent on our house to the company too. Well, the long and short of it is, by the end of the year, Pa owed more to the mine owners than he'd earned from working a ten-hour shift six days a week."

There was silence as the boys thought about this. "You think that's what expenses means?" Tony asked. "We get charged for food?"

"How could they charge us for that slop?" asked Ron in a pained voice. Nobody answered.

"Well, what would Schiner do with Eddie?" somebody else put in.

"Get rid of him," Luke replied. "That's what happened to troublemakers in our town. If somebody spoke out against the mine owners—even if they was just blowing off steam—they wound up in an accident. Found floating in the river or caught in the wrong place when some dynamite went off."

"You think Schiner . . . killed Eddie?" asked Tony.

"He mighta just driven him back to the highway and dumped him. It's twenty miles. You wouldn't want to walk it."

"But what would be the point?"

"To keep him from warning the rest of us, dummy," said Luke. "As long as we're willing to work, Schiner can use us. But if we get unhappy and start to make a fuss, then he'd have to get rid of us. Better not to let the rest of us know we're just working for three plates of grits and beans a day.

"Well, I'm through with that," said Ron. "I'm taking my stuff and getting out tonight. Who's with me?"

Tony hesitated. He could still see in his mind that stack of quarters he'd earned. He didn't want to let them go.

Nobody else jumped up to join Ron either. That took some of the wind out of his sails. "You all just gonna stay on here and work for nothin'?" he asked.

"At least we're eatin'," somebody said. "And we don't have to sleep under trees at night."

Tony had an idea. "Why don't we all just go together and ask Schiner about our money? If we stick together . . ."

"I'll go along with that," said Luke.

The rest of them reluctantly agreed. But when they knocked at the door of the main house, Schiner seemed friendly. "I know I owe you boys money," he said, "but I thought you'd stay till the end of the season. Truth is, I just haven't got the cash to pay you right now."

"What about the expenses?" asked Tony.

"Oh, I have a lot of expenses," said Schiner. "You boys don't realize how much it costs to run a farm. You have it easy."

"I don't mean that," Tony said. "I mean, what kind of expenses are you going to take out of our pay?"

"Well, I haven't got that figured out yet," Schiner replied. "See, if we get a good price for the crops, I might even let you boys all have a bonus. The ones that work for me till the end of the season, anyways."

Tony could see a few of the others nodding their heads, but he didn't believe Schiner. "What if we wanted to leave right now?" he blurted out.

In reply, he saw a mean look in Schiner's eyes that didn't match the soothing words. "Well, you go on if you want to," he said. "Nobody's keepin' you here."

"We can go, but we can't have our money."

"Tell you what," Schiner said smoothly. "I'll give you half what I owe you right now, and when you get settled write me with your address. I'll send you the rest when I sell the crop."

Tony didn't believe that for a minute. But he made up his mind that half the money was better than none. "I'll take it," he said.

Schiner peered at the others. "Anybody else want to give up the chance at a bonus and go back on the road?" he asked.

When nobody answered, Tony was surprised. He looked around. He expected Ron, at least, and maybe Luke to go with him. But Ron wouldn't meet Tony's eyes. He'd changed his mind. Luke glanced over and muttered, "I've had enough of the road."

Schiner smiled in a mean way, and Tony became a little afraid. He went back to the bunkhouse for his duffel bag. Nobody else said anything as he packed his few clothes and the copy of *Black Mask*, which was now tattered and missing a couple of pages. Tony knew most of the stories by heart, but he kept it because it reminded him of home.

As he walked back to the main house, his footsteps sounded awfully loud. He could smell roast chicken. That was what Schiner and his wife were having for supper. Tony stopped and peered through the lighted window of the farmhouse. Schiner was using a key to open a locked drawer in his desk. That must be where he keeps his money, thought Tony. He took a step closer, to see how much there was.

Then he saw Schiner take a pistol from the drawer, check to see if it was loaded, and put it in his pants pocket.

Tony felt as if his body were frozen. For a second, he couldn't move. Then he realized that he should get away from the window before Schiner saw him. Careful not to make any noise, he took a step backward. Then another.

If he ran, that might attract attention. Schiner's mean old black dog was tied up by the chicken coop. He barked at anything that moved in the nighttime.

Tony tried to clear his mind of the fear that numbed him. The only thing was to get away fast, before Schiner realized he was gone.

But where? There was only one road leading to the main road, and Schiner could easily catch Tony there with the pickup truck.

Then he thought of the cornfield. The plants were tall enough to hide him. When he reached the other side, he could run into the big woods. Schiner couldn't follow him in there.

Maybe. At any rate, it was the best plan he could think of. Fortunately, the moon was hidden behind clouds. That made it easier, except that Tony kept veering into the cornstalks, scraping his face and hands against the tough, sharp leaves. Once, he heard the dog barking, and that made him go faster. He dropped the duffel bag, and decided it wasn't worth going back for it.

Even without the bag, it took him forever to reach the far side of the field. He kept worrying that he had gotten turned around in the darkness, and would come out right back where he'd started. But finally he stumbled into the ditch that surrounded the field. He tripped and fell to his knees in the water at the bottom.

Trying to quiet his breathing, he listened. Far behind him, he could hear the sound of a truck engine. It was running pretty fast. Schiner must be looking for him.

Without hesitating, Tony pulled himself to his feet and plunged into the woods. Here it was almost completely dark. After running into a tree and tripping twice over branches lying on the ground, he realized he had to slow down.

He wished he'd paid closer attention when Schiner had brought him to the farm. Tony knew where the dirt road was, but he hadn't counted the number of turns they'd made in the truck after leaving the highway.

All he could do was to push on through the woods and hope he'd find a highway or railroad on the other side. Moving slowly, he began to notice noises all around him. Once or twice he heard an owl overhead. The other sounds, he hoped, were small animals like raccoons or rabbits.

Then he heard the sound of something that sounded large and heavy. Fortunately it was running away. A deer, Tony thought. That was all. The only things he really had to be afraid of were bears or wolves.

He stopped to listen. Something else had caught his ear. An engine. An automobile engine. Lots closer than before. But as Tony listened, it too went away from him.

Still, that meant there had to be a road close by. Tony thought some more. At night, all he could see of an approaching car would be its headlights. He wouldn't know if it was Schiner's truck or somebody else who might give him a ride.

Even though Tony's instincts told him to keep running, he decided it would be better to wait until morning. Lying down on the mossy ground, he wished he still had his duffel to use as a pillow. He tried to sleep, but every little noise in the woods made him sit up and listen.

Finally the sky overhead changed from black to gray. Around now, Tony thought, Schiner would be waking up the boys in the bunkhouse. They ate before the sun was up so they could use every bit of daylight for work time. Schiner probably would have given up looking for him.

So Tony headed toward the place where he'd heard automobiles passing last night. Another one went by as he approached now. Just before Tony came out of the woods, however, he heard barking.

He recognized it. It sounded just like Schiner's mean black watchdog. Just in time, Tony slipped behind a thick stand of tall bushes. Slowly he spread the branches a little.

Not far away, at the side of the highway, stood Schiner, holding the dog's leash in one hand and a shirt in the other. Tony recognized the shirt. It was his. Schiner must have found the duffel.

Trying to make himself invisible, Tony watched Schiner lead the dog down the road. He was trying to find a place where the dog could pick up Tony's scent.

Tony was lucky, for they were heading in the opposite direction from where he stood. He poked his head out a little farther. He could see Schiner's truck parked off to his right.

Tony hesitated. Schiner usually left his keys in the truck in case it had to be moved by one of the boys. But would he have done that now?

He took a deep breath. This was going to be dangerous, but he was desperate. Slowly, he came out from behind the bush. Schiner and the dog were about thirty yards away and looking in the other direction.

A few quick steps and Tony was on the other side of the truck. He peeked in the window and saw the keys dangling from the ignition lock. Without stopping to think about it, he opened the door and jumped inside.

As soon as he did, he heard a shout behind him. No need to wonder who that was. Tony released the hand brake and started the engine. Carefully he put the truck in gear. He prayed it wouldn't stall, the way it did sometimes when the driver started forward too quickly.

He let out the clutch pedal and the truck slowly began to chug forward. The engine coughed. Tony could hear the shouting and the dog barking—a lot closer now. He glanced in the sideview mirror and saw Schiner running. At first, he gained ground on the truck, but Tony pushed the gas pedal down and felt the truck lurch forward. With relief, he saw that Schiner was falling farther behind.

Then he heard a pistol shot and ducked. But nothing hit him. Shaking, he took another look in the rearview mirror. The last he saw, Schiner was jumping up and down and cursing in the middle of the road.

ELEVEN

Up in the Air

AUGUST 7–10, 1936

UNCLE GEORGIE WAS ANGRY. "I'M SURE MY HOTEL room was searched last night," he told Father. "I believe that we ought to report it to the police."

"It was probably the police who searched your room," Father told him. They were headed for the aerodrome in the Aldriches' old Opel. "After you cut off Hitler's speech, you're lucky they didn't throw you in jail."

"It was in the spirit of scientific research," Georgie replied.

David and his sister Esther were in the back seat of the car. Esther had been upset at having to leave her toys behind. She took only a small metal case filled with paper dolls and their clothes. David soothed her by describing how much fun going up in a balloon would be.

When they reached the aerodrome, Molly was waiting for them. She picked up Esther as though the little girl were a feather. "Ready to cross the ocean, little lady?" Molly asked.

"We're going to float in a balloon," Esther informed her.

"That one," said Molly, pointing toward the giant zeppelin that was being pulled out of its hangar with thick steel cables.

"Oh," said Esther, disappointed. "I thought it would be pink."

Molly turned to Father. "Have you notified Harry that we're going to bring him an instant family?"

"I sent him a telegram," said Father. "But I received no reply. Perhaps it would be better if David and Esther stayed at Aldrich House in Maine."

"I don't think that's a good idea," said Molly. "They haven't had any children there in a long time. I think it would be a gloomy place for your two."

"Do they still put on the play every summer?" Father asked.

"The older generation keeps up the tradition," Molly told him. "But it doesn't draw the crowds it used to. If your brother Harry would appear in the play, it would be a big help. But his film career has kept him too busy."

"How about Nell?" Father asked. "Could she take the children if Harry can't?"

"I doubt it," Molly told him. "She's cut herself off from the world, in that big house of hers in Santa Monica. She was shattered when the public didn't like her in talking pictures. People say she's very strange now."

"Maybe when Sara and I come over, we can visit her."

"Well, I hope you don't wait too long. These Nazis scare me," said Molly.

"Within a year at the latest," said father.

David didn't like leaving his parents. But Mother told him he had to be brave so Esther wouldn't be afraid. When he saw the big airship—which looked even bigger now that it was on the ground—he forgot his own fear. Uncle Georgie had told David it was the most exciting ride he would ever have. And something that was so big couldn't possibly be dangerous.

The *Hindenburg* was the very latest in zeppelin airships, with passenger rooms as luxurious as any hotel's. After a last hug good-bye from Father, they walked out toward the ship. A folding aluminum staircase led from the ground up into the linen-covered bag.

Inside, they stood in a long corridor. A white-coated steward examined their tickets. "This is B deck," he said. "The bar and smoking room are at the far end. Shower rooms are on your left. Atten-

Dining room of the Hindenburg

dants will provide you with fresh towels at any time. Your staterooms are upstairs on A deck."

They walked up another flight of stairs and found their rooms. David and Uncle Georgie were sharing one, and Molly and Esther another. David saw only a sofa, a desk, and a chair inside the room. He was puzzled until Georgie showed him the beds that folded into the walls during the daytime. The room also had its own small bathroom with a toilet and sink.

"The ship has twenty-four-hour room service," said Georgie. He pointed to a button on the wall.

"That bell will bring a steward who will take our order for food, drink, playing cards, or anything else we might need. Of course, there is a dining salon where we can eat our regular meals."

David heard a humming noise and felt the floor vibrate slightly. "The ship is going to lift off," said Georgie. "Let's go to the observation deck."

Other passengers had already gathered there. Molly lifted Esther onto her shoulders so she could see. The ground crew had released the cables, which were being pulled up into the ship. Very slowly, the zeppelin floated upward, and the figures on the ground became smaller. David saw Father standing by the Opel, waving.

"Up in the air!" Esther sang out gaily. The other passengers laughed.

David had one question for Uncle Georgie: "What will make the ship come back down?"

"There are valves for releasing some of the hydrogen," he said. "If the ship needs to rise higher or faster, the crew can open water tanks that provide ballast, or weight."

David could see the propellers on the ship's tail fins start to turn. The *Hindenburg* straightened out and headed west. The whole city of Berlin lay below them. David realized with sadness that he might not see it again for a long time. There were other cities in America, but he didn't think they would be like Berlin.

David had taken an airplane ride once. Riding in a zeppelin was very different. There was almost no noise, for one thing. And there was very little sense that you were moving fast. Though Uncle Georgie told David the airship traveled at 135 kilometers (84 miles) per hour, it seemed to drift as lazily as a cloud.

The most important difference between a zeppelin and an airplane was that you weren't confined in a cramped little seat. The ship had a library, a large dining room, and several observation decks where the passengers could sip drinks while watching the scenery.

It was twilight when they came in sight of the English Channel. The ship chased the setting sun, and the water below glittered as if it were on fire. David leaned against the window of the deck, trying to catch a glimpse of the white cliffs of England that he had read about.

An older man sitting next to Uncle Georgie remarked, "In the next war, the Channel will no longer be Britain's safety moat. Airships like these will bring Germany the victory she was cheated out of in 1918."

"I don't think there will be a war," Uncle Georgie replied. "Both sides would lose too much. People haven't forgotten the terrible cost—millions of young men—in the Great War. That was less than twenty years ago."

"This time," the man said firmly, "it will be different. Germany didn't have a leader like Hitler before."

David turned to look at the man. He seemed full of confidence. His eyes sparkled as if he were predicting a bright, happy future. One in which Germany would be the ruler of Europe.

"And now that zeppelins and airplanes can cross the Atlantic," the man continued, "the Americans cannot interfere. Unless they, too, want to suffer."

Uncle Georgie stood up. "We Americans licked you before, and we can do it again if we have to." He stalked off. Several other passengers had heard him, and stared angrily at his back as he left.

At dinner, word of Uncle Georgie's outburst had spread. The other passengers—mostly Germans—turned their heads away as he passed. "What have they got against you?" Molly asked as he and David sat down at a table with them. Georgie explained, and Molly smiled. "I agree completely, but since we have David and Esther along, maybe we'd better keep a low profile."

That was hard for Uncle Georgie to do. So he spent most of the rest of the voyage in his stateroom. He found out that he enjoyed ringing for the German stewards at odd hours, like three o'clock in the morning and asking for something like a toothbrush. The trouble was, David kept waking up whenever there was a knock at the door.

When morning came, David went out to the observation deck. Molly and Esther joined him. By now the ship was over the ocean, and he thought there wouldn't be much to see. He found out the scenery was more varied than he imagined. Cloud formations ahead of them changed colors as the sun passed through them. Every now and then the airship passed a ship bobbing on the ocean far below.

By mid-morning, however, the sky had grown steely gray. A steward informed the passengers that the ship was about to pass through a storm, but there was no need for anyone to worry.

Pretty soon, they heard a sound like small waves lapping against the side of the hydrogen-filled balloon. "That's what rain sounds like when you're this high up," a steward told them. In the distance, David saw a flash of lightning. "What happens if that strikes the ship?" he asked.

"The ship has lightning rods at both ends," the steward told him. "And the frame is made of aluminum, which will not attract lightning." Even so, David worried as the clouds closed in, reducing the view outside the windows to nothing but a massive gray fog. Once, a lightning bolt came so close that the sound of thunder made people clap their hands over their ears.

At last, the storm ended, and not long afterward they spotted land again. "Canada," Molly said. "We'll come down the coast to Maine in an hour. If we keep our eyes peeled, we might get to see Lake Chohobee, where Aldrich House is."

"Father once said it was a wonderful place to grow up," David said. "Could I visit there sometime?"

"You and Esther are great-grandchildren of Lionel Aldrich, the man who built the house," Molly told him, "so of course you'd be welcome. But we're going to California to find you a place to stay."

Maine seemed like the Black Forest of Germany, filled with dark fir trees and blue lakes. Molly pointed down once and said, "That's it. That's Lake Chohobee, and right at the lower end of it is Aldrich House." David looked, but there were too many lakes. He couldn't tell which one Molly was pointing at.

In a few hours, the airship was over New York City. Everyone crowded into the observation deck. The sight was breathtaking. Compared to Berlin, the buildings were sleek and new, glittering silver and white towers in the afternoon sun. To David, it looked like a picture from a book of fairy tales. He didn't understand how buildings that tall could stand up. Yet they looked so strong, as if they would stand forever. He was sure that nothing Germany could do would break them down.

Soon afterward, the *Hindenburg* finished its journey. Its pilot slid the metal nose of the airship into the top of a high metal pole. The crew tossed the metal cables to the ground, and workers pulled it close enough so the passengers could walk down the ladder again.

From there, the passengers boarded airplanes to other destinations. It was a disappointment to shift to the cramped seats and stuffy, small spaces of an airplane. Esther, who was usually sweet tempered, began to cry and complain. "I want to go home now," she insisted.

In the middle of the night, they reached Chicago, where they had to change planes. Uncle Georgie kept worrying whether his suitcase would get loaded onto the new plane. The trip to Los Angeles from Chicago seemed to take longer than crossing the Atlantic, even though it was less than half the distance. David kept trying to sleep, but he had nightmares that Hitler was chasing him because Uncle Georgie had stolen a zeppelin.

By the time they reached Los Angeles, the sun had risen again. Looking out the window of the plane as it landed, David saw palm trees and strange white birds. California was almost too bright and sunny.

They had expected Uncle Harry to send an automobile to meet them, but none appeared.

Molly had Harry's telephone number and found a pay phone. She looked amazed and then angry as she talked to the person who answered.

"Just like Harry," she said after she hung up. "He forgot we were coming. And what's worse, he said he doesn't have room for the children right now."

"Why not?" asked Uncle Georgie.

Molly glanced at David and his sister. Lowering her voice, she said, "I gathered from the background noise that a rather large party is going on. And in Harry's case that means it could last for a week."

David was impressed. How was it possible that his father—so serious and scholarly—could have a brother who held parties that lasted a week? "We could stay out of the way," he suggested hopefully. "We wouldn't bother anyone."

Molly said grimly, "No, Harry told me I should call Nell. He said she has loads of room."

"But she's . . ." Uncle Georgie began, and then trailed off.

"I know," said Molly. "But she's our last resort. I won't call her. We'll just take a taxi out there and bang on the door."

David wondered what Georgie had been going to say about Nell. That she was . . . what? Stingy? Mean to children? Crazy? He suddenly thought of a picture in a book he'd had when he was young. It showed the old witch who captures Hansel and Gretel and plans to eat them. But witches lived in dark places—forests and mountains. Here in Los Angeles it was so sunny that there couldn't be any witches.

Could there?

On Highway 66

AUGUST 9–10, 1936

TONY DROVE THE TRUCK UNTIL THE GAS GAUGE read empty. He kept checking the sideview mirror, because he knew Schiner would call the police as soon as he could.

Finally he saw a railroad station and parked the car next to it. He noticed that Schiner had left an old canvas jacket on the front seat. It was too hot to need one during the day, but Tony took it anyway. He figured Schiner owed him that much for a week's work. Tony could use it as a pillow at night, now that he'd lost his duffel bag.

Tony was hungry again, but he figured he ought to get farther away before he looked for food. As soon as a train stopped, he ran down the line of cars, looking for an open door.

That night, when the train stopped, Henry saw the flickering fires of a hobo camp near the tracks. Cardboard boxes and a few makeshift tents marked the places where people had made shelter to sleep in. He walked over there, his mouth watering from the smell of food cooking.

"How come so many hobos stopped here?" Tony asked a man who was cooking some strips of meat on a spit.

Hobo camp

"Railroad bulls got tough farther down," the man told him. "Amarillo Slim decided to keep all the 'bos out of Texas. He's the meanest bull there is."

The man noticed Tony staring at the meat. "Ever try that?" he asked. "It's raccoon. I'd rather have squirrel, but they're scarce around here."

Tony shook his head to clear it. "Is there any way to keep going west?"

The man gestured with his head. "Route 66 is over there," he said. "Stick out your thumb and hope a trucker picks you up. Follow it right smack into the Pacific Ocean."

Tony nodded. He'd have to find something to eat first. He felt his legs getting weak. He walked toward the lights of the little town and found a cheap-looking restaurant. But when he walked inside, the cashier stopped him. "You want a handout, go around to the back door," she said. "Maybe the cook will give you some leftovers."

Tony looked down at himself. His clothes were torn and filthy. He looked like the bums who went through the garbage cans in back of Pop's restaurant. He turned his head so the cashier couldn't see him cry.

Tony slept in an empty box that he found in back of a furniture store. But when he woke up he went back to the restaurant and washed dishes until the cook said he'd earned breakfast.

So when he walked up to Route 66 and stuck out his thumb, he felt pretty good. But the trucks roared by him without stopping. The sun rose higher in the sky, and his legs were tired. Tony heard the buzz of an airplane and looked up. That was the way to travel, he thought. He could be in Hollywood tomorrow if he had an airplane. He wondered if there was any way he could sneak onto one.

Discouraged, he began to walk, but the sun got hotter and he looked for a shady place to rest. Only there wasn't one. As far as he could see, not a single tree spread its green branches. In fact, in this part of the country just about everything that grew seemed to have shriveled up and turned brown.

Just then, he came over the top of the hill and saw smoke ahead. It looked like a car was on fire. A man and a woman were standing and watching it, but they didn't look like they were doing anything to stop it.

As Tony approached, he could see why. It was not a fire. The car's radiator had just overheated. Clouds of steam were coming out of the engine. Part of the trouble, he saw, was that the car was overloaded. A couple of mattresses and bedsprings were tied on top. Bits and pieces of furniture, cooking pots, and wooden boxes hung from the sides and rear. It looked like a junk shop on wheels.

The man and woman looked up when the saw him. Their eyes looked bleak, like somebody had drained all the life out of them. Tony felt as if he ought to just pass by, but somehow he couldn't do that.

"Looks like you got trouble," he said.

That brought the weakest of smiles to the man's face. "Son, trouble is *all* we got."

"Do you know anything about cars?" asked the woman.

"I told you," the man said softly. "I know what's wrong with it."

"A little," Tony replied.

By now the steam coming out had died down, and the man opened the hood of the car. It was a Model T Ford, one of the old ones they had stopped selling in 1927. Dirty brown water covered everything under the hood. The man reached down and pulled out what looked like a ragged and torn loop of rubber ribbon. "That's the trouble," he said. "Fan belt broke."

Tony remembered that the fan helped cool the engine. Without it, the water in the radiator overheated and turned to steam. "Guess we could get a new one," the man said slowly, "if we could find a garage."

Except for the water dripping out of the engine, there wasn't a sound. Tony thought there must not be a garage within miles. Then he realized that the man was looking at him—or rather, at the middle part of him.

Tony looked down. "You got a leather belt, I see," said the man.

Tony got the idea. He looked back and saw that the man's pants were held up with suspenders. Tony slipped the belt out of his pants loops and held it out. Then he reached down quickly because the pants were slipping. He hadn't realized how much weight he'd lost.

That made the woman smile. "You can get your belt back when we come to a garage," she said. "You going far?"

"To California," he told her.

"That's just where we're heading," she replied. "Why don't you find yourself a space in the backseat? Rae Ann, make a little room for this boy! What's your name?"

"Tony."

"Tony's going to sit next to you for a spell," she called through the window. "He's a real good-looking boy, so be nice to him, hear?"

Tony blushed and almost didn't get into the car. Then the woman leaned over and whispered in his ear. "Rae Ann's blind, you understand me? She's a little afraid of anything new. So I explain it to her first."

The girl in the backseat looked about ten. She was very thin; Tony could see the bones in her arms almost as if she had no skin. Blonde hair that was nearly white hung down over her face. She looked in his direction when he opened the car door. You couldn't tell from her blue eyes that she was blind, except that they seemed focused on something far away.

The woman got in the front seat and looked back at them. "I'm Cora French," she told Tony. "That's Henry fixing the engine."

Henry closed the hood and got behind the wheel. "That belt of yours fits just right," he said. "Pulled it up to the third notch and she was tight as a drum." He started the engine and the car shuddered. Everything tied onto the outside seemed to clang and rattle in protest as they started down the road.

The car ran pretty well until it came to a hill. Then it strained so much that Tony and the woman got out and pushed it till they reached the top.

Fortunately, there weren't too many hills. At last they pulled into a filling station. Henry talked to the owner for a while, and then came back to the car. "He says the fan belt for a Model T costs two dollars and thirty cents. That's a little steep for us." He looked at Tony. "I wonder if you'd mind we just go on using your belt? As long as we're all going in the same direction."

Tony shrugged. "Sure, I don't mind."

They filled the tank with gasoline and were off again. Rae Ann turned to Tony and asked, "Do you think everybody has a purpose in life?"

He was surprised. "Why . . . I guess I never thought about it."

"I think they do," she said, sounding very sure of herself. "And I try to guess what it is."

Tony nodded. Then he realized she couldn't see him and was waiting for an answer. "Uh-huh," he said.

"I think your purpose was to help us," she said. "We've had hard times, and now you came as a sign that's going to change."

The woman in the front seat turned around. "We lost our farm," she said. "Didn't have a drop of rain for the whole year, and the crops just dried up. Then the land had nothing to hold it together, and it turned to dust."

"And a great wind came up," the girl went on, "and blew the land away. The dust was so thick we nearly choked. Pa nearly got lost when he was out in it."

Her mother spoke up again. "Two of the Perkins boys—Elmer and Roy, Junior—they did get lost." She lowered her voice. "Went out in the dust storm and was never seen again."

Tony noticed that Henry never said anything when his wife and child talked about the farm. He just seemed to sink lower and lower into the front seat.

"So the bank wanted the payment for the mortgage," the mother said. "Well, of course there was no money. We hadn't even a weed to sell. Not a weed! Mr. Bradley, the banker, was real sorry about it. He gave us an extra day to pack up and leave after the bank auctioned off the farm."

"But I know it'll work out now," said Rae Ann. "Because Tony came along. That shows we're heading in the right direction."

What she said made Tony a little nervous, because he didn't think of himself as a messenger from God, or whatever Rae Ann imagined.

When night came Rae Ann tried to stretch out and sleep. Tony folded the jacket he'd taken from Schiner's truck and said she could use it for a pillow. But when she put her head on it, she gave a little cry.

"There's something hard inside it," she said.

"Rae Ann's real sensitive," her mother explained. "Just like the princess and the pea."

Tony unfolded the jacket and reached inside the pocket. His fingers closed on a smooth piece of metal, and some paper. When he realized what it was, he slipped it into his pants pocket. In the darkness, nobody noticed.

Rae Ann soon went to sleep, but Tony sat watching the dim headlights blaze a little path ahead of the car. Finally, Henry spotted a rest area and pulled off the highway. The car park was already full of other cars that looked like theirs—owned by uprooted families bringing all they had with them. Some had pitched tents on the grass; others just slept in their cars or trucks.

A lightbulb marked the place where the outhouses were. Tony excused himself and went inside one of the wooden stalls. Barely enough light to see by shone through the cracks in the door.

He took out the object that had bothered Rae Ann. It was a silvery money clip, holding a folded pack of dollar bills—ones, fives, and even a few tens. As he counted it, Tony's hands shook. It came to $116.

He didn't know what to do. So he counted it again.

Finally, he went back to the car. Both Henry and Cora were already asleep, and Rae Ann was now stretched out completely on the backseat. So Tony climbed on top of the car and lay down on the mattresses tied there. It was the most comfortable bed he'd slept in since the night he left Chicago. As he lay on his back, the stars appeared. He counted them. The total always came out to 116.

The next morning they got started early. The sun rose behind them, turning the road ahead into a rosy ribbon. Mrs. French opened a paper bag and took a couple of doughnuts from it. She offered one to Tony. He found that it was stale and hadn't been too good even when it was fresh. "These are good for traveling," Mrs. French said, as if she could read his mind. "Because they don't spoil so fast."

As soon as they saw a roadside restaurant, Tony told Henry to pull over. "I can pay for breakfast," Tony said. They protested, but not very much.

Inside, Rae Ann smiled as she smelled the plate of bacon and eggs the waitress put in front of her. "You see, Mama?" she said. "I knew Tony was sent to help us."

Finding Nell

AUGUST 15, 1936

THE FRENCH FAMILY STOPPED AT SAN BERNARDINO, when Henry saw a sign that read, "Fruit Pickers Wanted." They went down a dirt road to a big orchard. A man was handing out baskets and promising to pay 25 cents for each basket that they filled with peaches.

"I think I'll keep on going," Tony told the Frenches. "From what they said at the last filling station, it's only about fifty more miles to Los Angeles. I ought to be able to reach it by nightfall if I can hitch a ride." He shook hands with Henry and Cora.

"Do you want your belt?" Cora asked.

For the past few days, Tony had been using a rope to cinch up his pants. He decided it would do for now. "You need it more than I do," he said.

"We surely are grateful," Cora said. "For the belt and for the good meals. You can see it's made Rae Ann take on a little weight already."

"I know," Tony said.

"I'll pay you back when I can," Henry said.

"No need," Tony replied. "You brought me to California. That's what I needed."

He went over to the car to say good-bye to Rae Ann. "I knew you couldn't stay with us forever," she said. "There's probably a lot of other families who need helping."

"There sure are," he said. They had seen a lot of them on the road.

For the past few days, he'd been thinking about what he planned to do now. He took the money from his pocket. There was still over $100. Keeping $5 for himself, he put the rest in Rae Ann's hand.

"What's this?" she asked.

"Money," he told her. "Don't show it to your parents till they need it."

With her other hand, she reached out to touch Tony's face. Her fingers traced the outlines of it. "Now I won't forget you ever," she said.

"Rae Ann, you gave me something too," he said.

"What?"

"A feeling like I did something right."

On the highway, it didn't take long before a car stopped for Tony's outstretched thumb. Maybe his luck had changed. The driver soon told Tony his name was Burns. He was a salesman. "I go all over California and the West," he said. "Helps me stay awake if I've got somebody in the car to talk to. Course I can always talk to myself, but then . . ." He tapped his forehead. ". . . people may start to wonder if I'm a little batty. Know what I mean?"

"Yes," said Tony. He already feared the salesman was a little batty.

"Open that box there," Mr. Burns said, indicating a broad cardboard container on the front seat. Tony did, carefully, wondering if there was anything dangerous inside. But it only contained a lot of smaller boxes, bright red with white letters: E-Z TOOTHPASTE SAVER.

"That's what I'm selling," said Mr. Burns. "Take a look. Clever little gizmo. You know how it's always hard to get all the toothpaste out of the tube? Because people squeeze it in the middle, that's why. Well, the tube just fits into this, and you crank it up whenever you brush your teeth. Keeps all the toothpaste in the top of the tube till the very end." He smiled, waiting for Tony's reaction. Tony nodded and said it was a good idea.

"Good?" Mr. Burns said. "It's what this country needs right now—a product that everybody wants and could afford to buy. Like the Model T Ford was in the twenties, know what I mean? If even half the people in the country buy one, that would put more people to work making and selling them. And pretty soon . . ." He snapped his fingers. ". . . the country is back on its feet again. I'll sell you that whole boxful for two dollars. That's less than a dime apiece."

"I wouldn't need more than one," said Tony. "And I don't even have any toothpaste," he added. The man made you feel like you should have one of these, all right.

"No, see, the idea is, you go into business," said Mr. Burns. "There's twenty-four in that box. You sell 'em to other people. Maybe for a quarter. Fifty cents if you can get it. Say a quarter apiece. Then you'd have six dollars. See how easy that is? Start with two dollars, turn it into six dollars in less than a day. I'll give you my card if you have to order more. Opportunity of a lifetime."

"I don't think so," said Tony. "I've got to get someplace."

Mr. Burns didn't seem discouraged that Tony had turned down the opportunity of a lifetime. "Where you headed?"

"Hollywood, I guess," Tony replied. "I'm looking for a movie star."

"Oh, they don't live in Hollywood, kid. That's just where the studios are. You know what you need? A map that shows where all the stars live."

Tony nodded. "That's right. That would be great."

"Look in that green box on the backseat," said Mr. Burns. "I used to sell those maps on the corner of Hollywood and Vine. There's about twenty left. I'll let you have the whole lot for a dollar fifty."

Mr. Burns finally dropped Tony off at Santa Monica Boulevard. Tony had paid him a dime for one map. From the map Tony had found out that Nell Aldrich lived at 1717 San Vicente Boulevard. "That's near the beach," Mr. Burns told him. "Wait here until the number 32 Pacific Electric comes along. A bright red streetcar. It'll take you down to Ocean Front Boulevard, and it's a short walk to San Vicente."

Tony had figured out all the directions and reached the coast. A breeze was blowing in from the ocean, and he bought a hot dog from a cart on the boardwalk. He ate as he walked, wondering what he was going to say to Nell Aldrich after coming all this way. If Nell didn't remember his father, what was Tony going to do next? He remembered the business card in his coat pocket. He could buy some toothpaste savers and go into business.

Pacific Electric streetcar

San Vicente Boulevard wasn't very busy. All the houses were set way off from the road, sometimes with high fences. Up ahead, Tony saw a boy about his age sitting on a stone wall, his feet dangling above the ground. And there, right at the gate in the wall, was a mailbox. Written on it was: ALDRICH 1717.

Tony stopped. He looked at the boy. The boy looked back. "What kind of wurst is that?" asked the boy, who had a German accent.

"It's . . . a hot dog," said Tony.

"They make it from dogs?"

"Of course not." But Tony wondered. He did not actually know why it was called a hot dog. In the restaurant, his mother made sausages from pork, but they weren't hot dogs.

"I am David Aldrich," said the boy. "I am pleased to meet you."

"I'm Tony Vivanti. Are you Nell's son?"

David shook his head. "She has no husband or children. My sister and I are only visiting–not long, I hope."

"Why's that?" asked Tony. "Isn't she rich? You must have everything."

David shrugged. "Have everything, yes. But that does not make anyone happy. I would not have guessed that before. Now I know it is true. I was just sitting here wondering . . ." He paused, and then decided Tony could keep a secret. ". . . thinking I would escape, run away you know. See some of the country."

"Well, I just did," Tony told him. "Take it from me, it's no picnic."

"Did you come from far away?"

"Chicago. My father has a restaurant there. He always says he was friends with this Nell Aldrich. I thought I'd come out and see."

David smiled. "Good. Come in."

"You sure?"

David shrugged. "If she gets angry, I will leave with you. You can show me how to survive."

David stuck out his hand, and Tony shook it. He wasn't sure he could show David or anybody else how to survive. But he followed David up the driveway, which wound through a grove of oak trees. They came to a large house that looked Mexican. It had white stucco walls, orange roofs, and walkways made of colorful glazed tiles.

David led him around to the back. An Asian-looking man was working in a garden filled with flowers. Tony's mouth opened as he looked at the dazzling colors. His grandfather had taught him a lot about plants, but he couldn't name most of the flowers he saw.

"I don't like that one," came a voice from above. Tony looked up. A woman stood on a second-floor balcony, directing the gardener. "Take the pink ones away, Kenji," she said, and then noticed David and Tony. She shaded her eyes with her hand.

"Rocco?" she said in a disbelieving voice. "Rocco? Is that you?"

Tony realized she was looking at him. "I'm Tony," he said. "Rocco is my father."

"Oh." She sounded disappointed. "You're dirty, though. Just like Rocco was."

That irritated Tony, even though he had to admit he was dirty. "My father isn't dirty anymore," he said. "He dresses better than most of the people I've seen."

"I guess that's why he sent you out to me," she went on.

"He didn't send me," said Tony. "I just came to see you. I'm leaving now."

He turned his back and took a few steps, but she called after him. "What's your hurry? We're going to have lunch soon. Besides, it's dangerous outside."

He faced her again. "Dangerous? How do you know?"

"Oh, I listen to the radio," she said. "I read the newspapers. Even though people don't like me anymore, I know what's going on."

Tony glanced at David, who just shook his head.

"David," Nell went on as if it were already decided, "get Tony cleaned up."

A Mexican woman served them lunch on what Nell called the veranda. Tony felt different after he had a shower and a change of clothes. "I want to ask you something," he said to Nell. "Why do you think people don't like you anymore?"

"They don't," she said firmly. "They wouldn't come to my movies. And your father. I wanted him to come out here and live. 'Bring your wife, your children,' I told him. 'I have plenty of money.' But he wouldn't."

"He likes the restaurant business," said Tony. "He'd be unhappy if he had nothing to do."

"We have plenty to do," Nell said. "Ask David. I have all the latest games. We played Monopoly for hours last night."

"You have to let her win or the game won't stop," David told Tony in a low voice.

"I heard that," Nell said. "Well, it's my house, isn't it? I can win if I want to. Everything can be exactly as I want it."

Tony stared at her. "No," he said.

"Yes, it can," she said, pressing her lips into a little pout.

He took a deep breath. "There are people all over the country who barely have enough to eat."

"Oh, I know that. But what can I do about it?"

He thought. "You could make a movie about them. Show what's going on."

"You sound like my sister Peggy," Nell said. "She wants to do that. She goes around and makes documentary movies of people standing in line for food, or losing their homes because they can't afford to pay for them. The movies she makes are all very sad." Nell took a small bite of a cucumber sandwich. The cook had cut the crusts off it first.

"But I can't do that," Nell went on. "People don't like me. I tell you what. Let's play a game of miniature golf after lunch. I have my own course."

"You have to let her win at that too," said David.

"Don't you ever go out?" Tony asked.

"Certainly I do," she said. "Whenever I want to look at the ocean, Alfred drives me down there. Then we come back."

"You can walk there in ten minutes," said Tony. "And you can swim too."

"But there are people on the beach," she said. "People I don't know. It's dangerous."

Tony stared at her. She was crazy, he thought. Probably he should get out of here and go sell toothpaste savers. Then he thought of something. "Do you think everybody has a purpose in life?" he asked.

She pursed her lips and wrinkled her forehead. "Of course," she said. "They must have."

"What is yours?" he asked.

She looked annoyed. "I don't know," she said after a long pause. "What do you think it is?"

"I guess I came here to help you figure it out," he told her.

She laughed. It was a nice sound, Tony thought. And when she smiled, she looked beautiful to him. She could still be a movie star if she wanted, he thought.

That evening, they listened to President Roosevelt on the radio. Nell didn't want to, but Tony promised that if she would, he'd play Monopoly when the speech was over.

Back home, Pop always used to make everybody listen whenever Roosevelt spoke on the radio. Tony didn't understand why, but when people heard the president, they usually felt a little better. He hoped that would work with Nell too.

He looked at her. She pretended not to pay any attention at first. But then something Roosevelt said made her smile. Pretty soon, she was nodding as if she agreed with what the president was saying.

Tony thought about everything that had happened to him in the last three weeks. The people he'd met . . . if only he could show them to Nell. She'd understand that she couldn't stay cooped up here behind her walls playing games. She was wasting her life. Maybe Rae Ann was right. Maybe Mr. Burns was right too. Tony did have a purpose, an opportunity to do something important. He was supposed to come all this way to wake up Nell. He chuckled to himself when he thought what Pop would say.

David was listening too. He didn't understand all the words, but Roosevelt's voice made him feel

President Roosevelt

good. It filled the room like sunlight on a cold day. America was lucky to have Roosevelt and not Hitler, David thought. Hitler made people angry and afraid. But Roosevelt . . . just listening to him made you think that tomorrow was going to be better than today. He could relax tonight. He could even go ahead and play this Monopoly game. Because everything would somehow be all right.

A Few Historical Notes

During the Great Depression of the 1930s, the United States experienced the longest and worst economic time in its history. Millions of people lost their jobs and sometimes their homes and farms. Like Tony, many men and boys—and sometimes women and girls too—boarded freight trains, hoping to find a better life somewhere else. You can read about them in *Riding the Rails: Teenagers on the Move During the Great Depression*, by Errol Lincoln Uys.

President Franklin D. Roosevelt established a series of agencies to help deal with the Depression. One of these was the Civilian Conservation Corps (CCC). It opened about 1,500 camps for young men over the age of 17, paying them $30 a month plus food, clothing, and housing. In return, the men worked at conservation and public-works projects, like planting trees, building roads and walls, and stocking fish in streams and rivers. You can read about the CCC and the Depression in *A Nation in Torment*, by Edward Robb Ellis.

Adolf Hitler became chancellor of Germany less than two months after Roosevelt became president of the United States. Germany, too, suffered from economic hard times. Hitler blamed Jewish bankers and business owners, thus gaining support for anti-Semitic laws that would eventually result in the Holocaust, in which six million Jews were killed. Among the Jews who fled Germany at this time were scientists like Albert Einstein. However, the United States had cut off the flow of immigration in the 1920s, and turned away many thousands of Jews who hoped to find refuge here.

Hitler hoped that the 1936 Olympic Games in Berlin would be a showcase for Nazi Germany and its "Aryan" athletes, a supposed master race with Nordic features. (German Jews were not allowed on the German Olympic team.) However, the success of African-American athletes like Jesse Owens showed that "Aryans" with their fair skin and blonde hair were not racially superior to non-Aryans. You can read about the 1936 Games in *Hitler's Olympics*, by Duff Hart-Davis. *The Complete Book of the Olympics*, by David Wallechinsky, has the story of what American gold-medal winner Helen Stephens said to Hitler.

The invention of television was the work of many people. Two of the Americans who made key contributions to television broadcasting were Philo T. Farnsworth and Russian immigrant Vladimir K. Zworykin. Television broadcasting began in Great Britain in late August 1936, but few people had receivers, or TV sets. In the United States, widespread use of television in homes did not come until the early 1950s.

All the details in our story about the zeppelin airship *Hindenburg* are true. The *Hindenburg* itself exploded into flames while docking at Lakehurst, New Jersey, on May 6, 1937. Thirty-six people were killed in the spectacular blaze, which was recorded on motion-picture film and later shown in theaters around the world. The disaster discouraged further development of the hydrogen-filled zeppelins. The blimps that are used for advertising purposes today are filled with non-flammable helium and do not have rigid metal frames. You can read about the *Hindenburg* in *The Hindenburg*, by Michael Mooney.

Amelia Earhart disappeared over the Pacific Ocean on her attempt to fly around the world in 1937. The mystery of exactly what happened to her and her navigator, Fred Noonan, has never been solved. You can read about it in our earlier book, *Vanished*.

The Vivanti Family

m

Rocco (1900–)   Teresita (1902–)

Tony (1923–)   Leo (1924–)   Gabriella (1932–)

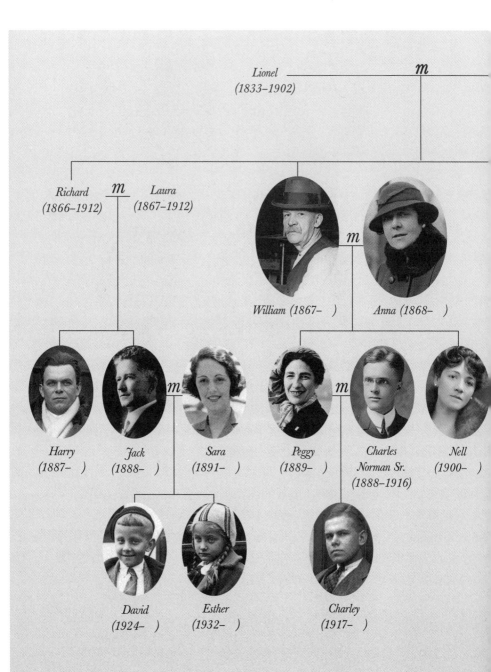

Lionel
(1833–1902) m

Richard m Laura
(1866–1912) (1867–1912)

m

William (1867–   )   Anna (1868–   )

Harry   Jack   m   Sara   Peggy   m   Charles   Nell
(1887–   )   (1888–   )   (1891–   )   (1889–   )   Norman Sr.   (1900–   )
                                                                                (1888–1916)

David   Esther   Charley
(1924–   )   (1932–   )   (1917–   )

Family

Adele
(1838–1910)

Zena
(1840–1919)

m

Maud (1872–)   Nick Woods (1870–)   George (1874–)

Molly
(1898–)

Polly
(1898–)

Freddy
(1899–)

Things that Really Happened

1930

The first packaged sliced bread appears in stores: Wonder Bread.

General Foods introduces Birds Eye Frosted Foods to grocery stores in Massachusetts. Developed by Clarence Birdseye, these are the first frozen foods sold to the public.

United Airlines hires the first airplane stewardess, Ellen Church.

1931

The George Washington Bridge, then the world's longest suspension bridge, is completed, connecting New York and New Jersey across the Hudson River.

The Chrysler Building and the Empire State Building are completed in New York City.

President Herbert Hoover signs a bill making "The Star-Spangled Banner" the national anthem.

1932

The automobile industry suffers its worst year of the Depression. General Motors sells a total of 5,810 automobiles in 1932, about the same as its weekly total in 1929.

Veterans of World War I, who never received the bonus money they were promised for serving in the war, organize a protest march on Washington, D.C. About 20,000 veterans camp out in parks around the nation's capital. On July 28, U.S. Army troops led by General Douglas MacArthur drive out the "Bonus Army" by using tear gas and bayonets.

During the Years 1930–1939

Franklin Delano Roosevelt defeats Herbert Hoover in the presidential election.

1933

As Roosevelt takes the oath of office in March, about 25 percent of all working-age Americans are unemployed.

On March 12, Roosevelt gives his first "fireside chat," speaking directly to Americans over the radio.

Frances Perkins becomes the first woman Cabinet member when Roosevelt names her secretary of labor.

During the first hundred days of his administration, Roosevelt pushes through Congress many new programs designed to help Americans suffering from the economic Depression. This is the beginning of the New Deal, the name for Roosevelt's domestic program, which improved the nation and helped its people in ways that are still felt today.

The first drive-in movie theater opens in Camden, New Jersey.

In December, the Twenty-First Amendment to the Constitution is ratified, repealing the Eighteenth Amendment. Alcoholic beverages are once again legal under federal law.

1934

Nabisco Company introduces Ritz Crackers, which were so popular that the company sold five billion of them in the first year.

Dust storms sweep the Plains states, removing about 300 million tons of topsoil.

1935

President Roosevelt creates the National Youth Administration (NYA) to provide jobs for young people.

The Social Security Act becomes law, creating a national system of old-age pensions and disability benefits.

The Cincinnati Reds host the Philadelphia Phillies in the first major-league baseball night game. From the White House, President Roosevelt throws a switch that turns on the artificial lights at Crosley Field in Cincinnati.

Howard Johnson opens his first roadside restaurant in Boston, Massachusetts.

Roosevelt establishes the Rural Electrification Administration to bring electric power to rural areas that previously have not had it.

1936

Roosevelt defeats Alfred M. Landon of Kansas in the presidential election. The victory of the Democratic Party in Congress is the largest ever, leaving only 89 Republicans (out of 435) in the House of Representatives and 16 (out of 96) in the Senate.

1937

The Golden Gate Bridge, still the world's longest suspension bridge, is completed near San Francisco.

The Hormel Company introduces the canned meat Spam.

Walt Disney and his artists make *Snow White and the Seven Dwarfs*, the first full-length animated motion picture.

On June 22, Joe Louis knocks out Jim Braddock to become boxing's heavyweight champion.

1938

In a Halloween night broadcast, Orson Welles and the Mercury Theatre present "Invasion From Mars."

Because the radio play uses made-up news broadcasts as part of its script, many listeners mistakenly believe that Martians have landed in New Jersey.

Superman, a comic book character, makes his first appearance in *Action Comics*. He is the creation of two teenagers, Jerry Siegel and Joe Shuster, but they sign a contract that gives the profits to the comic book publisher.

1939

The Department of Agriculture begins distributing food stamps to help the needy buy food.

General Electric introduces fluorescent lights.

The first Little League baseball league is formed in Williamsport, Pennsylvania.

Albert Einstein writes President Roosevelt a letter, pointing out that it is possible to build an atomic bomb more powerful than any weapon in history. Einstein, a Jew who fled Nazi Germany, fears that Germany may be working on such a bomb.

A presidential proclamation sets the date for Thanksgiving as the fourth Thursday in November, instead of the last Thursday. The purpose is to provide a longer Christmas shopping season to help retail stores.

Pocket Books introduces the first paperback editions of popular and classic books.